KEEP IT
ON THE DOWN LOW

To: Ms. Ollie,

Thank you for all the love and genuine concern and support. I love your spirit. I thank God for you. May He keep you & continue to Bless you!

Love

Gwen

KEEP IT
ON THE DOWN LOW
by
Allysha Hamber

Published by:
Voices Books & Publishing
P.O. Box 3007
Bridgeton, MO 63044
www.voicesbooks.homestead.com

Printed in the United States of America

Library of Congress Catalog Card No.: On File

ISBN: 0-9776992-0-X

SHOUTS OUT...

First and foremost, giving all honor to God. Thank You for Your grace, which is freely given to those like me who don't deserve it. Thank you for the ability to take simple words and create a novel.

Secondly, I'd like to thank those who believed in me when no one else would, including myself. My "Mother-in-Christ," Regina Lockhart, my nana Gracie Brewer, my God-Parents (KC and Patricia Brown), Mrs. Childress (thanks for sincerely caring...), Mrs. Pargo (Hi my Mrs. Pargo!), Ms. Paige (so feisty all the time!) and Ms. Terri Woods (crazy as hell!) I love you all and I genuinely thank you for your support!

A loving thanks to Mr. Carlos Whitby, Kevin Ivory-Bey, Darrell Jackson, and Jason Lambert. To the following individuals at the FMC Carswell...Ms. Alice Johnson, Frieda Harris, Evelyn Wilson, Frieda Douglass, and Ms. Sharon Stewart, thanks so much.

Thanks to the following people at FPC Lexington...Patricia Lyles, Roberta Deets, Taleshua Platt, Anitra Brabson, Cassie Armstrong, Lisa Boraders, Jackie Lawrence, Faye Scales, April Cline (a heartfelt thanks, wherever you are), Robin McCoy, Deborah Robinson, Shirley Delaney, Tina Evans Jerleane McNeil, Ella Royal and Mrs. Rosie Harless.

My co-workers Desmond, Danny, Mike, Tyrone, Roscoe and Jeff Pedrotty, thanks for all the support. The *X-treme* softball players and their families...Mike and Angie Randle, Chuck and Judy Haynes, Janet and Darren Cooper, Demetrius, Reggie, James, Jack, Yogi, Ya-Ya, Lil Mike and Moe. You're still the baddest team in the land in my book.

Ms. Dee Dee Mason, you know I love me some Dee Dee (smile). Thank you, for allowing me to be apart of your life. Love ya!

A SPECIAL THANK YOU

A special thanks to Mrs. Brenda Hampton for all her encouragement, love and genuine support. It's so nice to see a sistah who's truly real! God truly blessed me when he brought you into my life. My mother Ozella Foster Robinson, much love. Derick "Kidd" Stevenson, thank you for all you've been to me. My little-*BIG* brother Chris a.k.a Big Slug, you gonna do big things in life, I just know. My little God brother Antonio, I wish you well in everything you set out to do. I love you! My sister LaNelle, you ready to carry those bags yet? (Smile) No, seriously though, thanks for all the love, fussing and support over the years, I love you! My niece Taderra (America's next top model) you know you're my baby. Quionna (Raven's future replacement), Miracle (WNBA, here we come)! My nephews CJ, Cory and Chris (let's take the sports world by storm)! My god-daughter Ce-Ce, I know I've been busy but know that I love you still. Punkin (the Big Girl), Rhonda, Wayne Jackson, Alfred Pugh (I Love you so much. You know you'll always have a very special place in my heart), Vincel, Robin Foster, Tony Fisher, ShaTonya Green, Aunt Mary, Aunt Poochie and all my family, whose love means so much to me, "Thanks."

To my star on the cover Shannon Rucker, A.K.A, Ms. Hollywood. You all ready know how beautiful I think you are. "Thank you" for taking this book to a whole new level. I love you!

Sandra Mattox, what can I say…still bluer than the ocean blue…love you! And last but certainly not least, Simone Lowe. My "Mon'e in the middle," Always hyped about every chapter. You have been blue since day one. Never changing, always encouraging….thank you from the bottom of my heart.

- Love Always, Allysha

PRELUDE

It had been a messed up day all around. It began that morning with target practice out at the range. We were trying to get our Howitzers (military guns) on line and firing without the help of our Section Chief and my best friend Cory. He was restricted to the barracks due to testicle removal. Blue balls they say...serves him right. Hell, I'm surprised his jimmy didn't fall off with it. But that's my main man. Would give my life for him at the drop of a dime cause I know he would do the same for me.

Anyway, we couldn't get our guns on line and we misfired and hit the left corner of the local Dallas-Fort Worth airport lot. Thank God it was the middle of the night and "somewhat" deserted. I was temporarily in charge, so I caught most of the heat from the BC (Battalion Commander). He yelled, cussed, turned red as hell and cussed some more. Told me I couldn't find my way to my asshole without a "seeing-eye-dog." Sprinkled spit everywhere as he said it. Yeah, I'd say he was pretty pissed. I was gonna be reprimanded. He'd see to that. Company grade Article 15. Most likely a reduction in rank and a pay cut. Hopefully just extra duty. Money was funny and the bills were laughing as it was.

We were supposed to stay at the range overnight but the BC was so pissed, he called the entire exercise off until further notice. He made promises of very late work nights and extra duty to keep us busy until then. Fine by me. I just wanted to get home and cuddle up with my baby Alicia. We'd been going through some rough waters lately and I wanted to surprise her with a night of quality time and passion.

I stopped by Taylor's all night florist on Broadway and Fourth St. and picked up a dozen white, long stemmed roses. They were her favorite. Signed the card, "All My Love," cause that's what she had. I then swooped by the Class Six Liquor store and bought a bottle of Alize'. Tonight, I would rely on him like Viagra, trying not to let the thoughts of past mistakes override the love I felt for my woman and the feeling of the pleasure inside her walls.

I hit Hwy 35 home while listening to Babyface's, "Never Keep a Secret," on the radio. "...I never meant to lie to you but I needed me an easy way out..."

For a moment I allowed my thoughts to drift back to the secret that almost cost me the one I love. I quickly shook them away as I pulled onto my street. Cory's black and silver Isuzu jeep was parked in the driveway behind Alicia's metallic green Geo storm. He'd probably stopped by to keep her company. Make sure she was safe. Busta's around these military bases know when you're deployed and your families are home alone. Good lookin' out "C", but now you gots to take yo' ass home cause I'm about to handle my business.

I walked up the newly paved walkway and on to the porch. It was freshly painted a pale color of blue. An exact duplicate of the connecting home next door. That's the only thing I couldn't stand about military life. Everybody had all the same things because stores were so limited around the bases. Everyone's house looked the same. Everyone had the same furniture, the same cars and the same clothes. I could see how a drunk bastard could easily end up trying to enter the wrong front door.

I slipped my key inside the lock and pushed softly against the door. The living room and hallway lights were out inside. I walked towards the creme colored leather sofa and tripped over Cory's size eleven Lugz on the floor. I regained my balance and then proceeded to the kitchen to sat down the roses and Alize'. What the hell is goin' on up in here?

My heart raced like hell as I rounded the corner and headed for the bedroom. The off white door was slightly cracked, so I cautiously pushed it open. I saw Cory first. Propped up in my cherry oak framed waterbed, covers waist high, with pillows propped three deep behind him. His muscles staring back at me from his bare chest. Alicia was in the lounge chair beside the bed with her favorite Dallas Cowboys blanket thrown across her lap. Both were sound asleep. I softly tapped on the door and Alicia woke up. When she noticed it was me, her eyes lit up momentarily until she noticed the look on my face. She rose up, looked at Cory, and pulled the covers over his chest. That move made me a little jealous. As she came towards me she whispered, "When he stopped by he was running a fever, so I made him lie down." She threw her arms around me and inhaled my jungle like scent. "Ummm, that dirty oil smell I love so much."

She pulled back. "I thought you were gone until tomorrow?"

"We were, until we fucked around and blew up the airport."

Her eyes widened in disbelief.

"Don't worry, we didn't kill nobody," I quickly reassured her. "We hit a deserted back part of the lot. Since I was in charge, though, I probably got an Article 15 coming my way. If I can get this ol' limp nut nigga up on his feet and back to work, my days will be hella easier."

She placed her hand to my chest. "Stop it, Arman', he's really sick. Come on." She took me by the hand and led me into the living room. She grabbed the remote and turned on the TV to give us light and sat down upon my lap.

"So, how's my two favorite ladies," I asked rubbing my hand up and down the crease of her back.

"Well, I'm fine. And I don't know what makes you think that this is a girl. I want a boy," she said, rubbing her pumpkin sized belly.

"Alicia, I already have a son and..." Shit! I caught myself too late. I'd brought up the subject that was at the core of the distance between us. She quickly looked away from me and before I stuck my foot in my mouth any further, I raised her up and told her I'd be right back. She sat with her head in hands.

I went into the kitchen and poured Alicia a glass of apple cider. I grabbed the Alize' for me along with her roses. When I returned to the living room, I stood in front of her and as she raised her head, her eyes began to sparkle once again.

"I'm sorry baby. These are for you."

I handed her the roses as the tears fell from her eyes.

"Six for you and six for my baby boy."

She smelled the roses, laid them down on the table and reached for me. She pulled me down beside her, grabbed both my ears and planted a soft kiss on my lips. She slid her hands across my chest.

"Wanna share a shower?" she asked.

"Only if you don't mind the dirt."

As we rose and headed for the back she kissed me again. We entered the bedroom and we passed by Cory. I accidentally bumped the corner of the bed, waking him. He let out a dry, horse cough.

"Wake up with yo' sackless ass," I joked. "You need to hurry up and get yo' nutts in tact. Nigga, we fucked around and blew up the damn airport lot. Our computers were all messed up and you know Private Jackson didn't know his ear from his asshole. BC was kickin' ass and takin' names...mostly mine!"

Cory shook his head and tried to laugh. "Damn, playa. Just gimme a few mo' days and I'll be there to bail ya'll sorry asses outta trouble. Back at work, back on the town, back up in the guts of somebody's daughter!"

"Cory!" Alicia snapped.

"Sorry, LeLe," Cory said, as he reached over to answer the black cordless phone. His face tensed and I knew there was trouble on the line, maybe the BC. He looked to Alicia first, then to me.

"Phone dawg."

I looked at my watch. "Damn, playa, who dat?"

"Terri," he whispered.

AWWWW, DAMN! Here we go again...

CHAPTER 1

I met my lady Alicia at her job in the summer of '99. She was working at the AFFES Exchange on the Army base. I was a few months fresh out of basic training, and at my first duty station in Ft. Hood, TX. I noticed her every time I went into the store for something, anything. From the moment I first laid eyes on her, I was crazy about her. She would stand behind her register with her long, thick black hair blowing in the breeze from the mini fan mounted on her register. Her skin was smooth like caramel and her eye lashes were long and thick. She didn't wear any make-up, which for me was the beauty of it all. Her lips were full and in between them, lie the prettiest set of teeth you could imagine. I would wait and fumble around in the aisles until her line was empty so she could be the one to check me out.

When I lay in my bed, I would think about her sometimes at night, imagining us together. I lay there picturing her smile while, "Just my Imagination," played on the Quiet Storm. "...outta all the fellas in the world, she belongs to me. But it was just my imagination, once again, running away with me..."

Each time I saw her, she would greet me with a smile that would melt my heart. But, I was afraid to say anything to her. That was, until the day I stopped to buy a pack of cigarettes for Cory. She flashed those pearly whites at me and asked, "Are you old enough to be buying Benson & Hedges?"

"I sure hope so, but here, I'll show you my ID anyway." I took my military ID from my wallet and handed it to her.

She replied with yet another smile. "Nice picture."
I smiled then. After that day, when I would see her, we would speak and hold brief conversations. A couple of weeks later, I saw her at the Killeen mall with a couple of her friends. I was with Cory, and as usual, he spotted them first. He loved the ladies and had the scorecard to prove it. He heavily believed in, "love 'em and leave 'em." He hit me on the arm.

"Damn, dawg, look over there. Damn she fine! Baby got a set of hams on her! I'm about to go and get them digits."

"I know her dawg. She works at the Hood Rd. Exchange. We cool like that."

"Yeah well, I plan on being cool with them hams tonight."

"Nigga please, you ain't got no rap."

"She don't know that. Watch and learn. Let me show you how a real playa does it. "

I shook my head and followed his lead. We walked over to the Fredrick's of Hollywood store where they were shopping for lingerie. Cory stood in the doorway watching. They'd pick up pieces, confer with each other and put them back. Alicia picked up a silk and lace red teddy. I wondered who she would be wearing it for. Some lucky muthafucka no doubt. She placed it back down on the rack. I sucked my teeth and smiled. Yeah, that's right, fuck him.

When they exited the store, they walked towards Cory. All I could do was stare in amazement at how fine she was. Cory extended his hand to her, she accepted and they started talking. The conversation seemed to have her interest, at least until she noticed me standing off by the rail, watching them. She quickly released his hand and strolled over to speak to me.

"Hey you, what are you doing here?"

"Spending my paycheck, how about you?"

"Hanging out with my girls. You shopping alone?"

"Naw, Cassonova over there is my boy. I see you left him hangin", what's up with that." She smiled. "He wasn't talkin' about nothing. He still using those weak ass "drink yo' bath water" lines. A lil to played out for me. Besides, I'd much rather stand here and holla at my friend."

I smiled in return. "Oh, I'm yo' friend now?"

She laughed. "Yeah, I guess so. You seem aight."

I ran my hand down her arm. "I'm good peoples."

"So, what's up," she said, fidgeting with her fingers. I couldn't believe she was nervous.

"Nothing really. The question is, what are you getting into tonight," I asked, nodding towards the Fredrick's store.

She smiled a kinky smile. "You so silly, nothin' like that. We'll probably go to the club. How about you?"

"I don't club much, but if you'll be there, that's definitely a reason to be in the house."

"Oh really, then I guess I'll see you there." She turned to walk away then turned back to me. "We'll be at the NCO club. And don't spend all your money or you won't be able to get in."

"Oh, don't you worry, I'll be there."

As she walked away, I watched her walk. It was the first time I'd gotten a full scope of the bottom half of her body. It was indeed as fine as the top. Cory was right, she had a hella pair of hams on her and an ass to die for. Cory strutted towards me.

"Man, what's up with ol' girl, dawg? She tried to act like she wasn't feelin' me."

"Maybe, she's a lil too classy for yo' pimped out ghetto mackin' skills."

"Man whatever! I can have any ho I want. As soon as she left, I got both her girls phone numbers. And, I'll pull her cause can't no women resist me. I gots too much game."

"We'll see. She'll be at the NCO club tonight. But, I'm telling you "C", she way outta yo' league."

He just laughed and walked off. He has always been so full of himself and also his biggest fan.

That night, I must have changed gear I know about six times, trying to find something that stood out. My choice was finally a pair of heavily starched Fubu jeans, a starched Fubu jeans shirt and my low top white Nike's. I polished my Hawaiian gold tooth and cleaned my baby diamond studded earring. Before going to the mall I had my hair cut. But, I did trim my goatee.

There was a knock on the door. At the time, I was staying in the dormatory style, single soldier's barracks. A one-room hotel like setup. I had a queen sized bed, chest and dresser. A living room area equipped with a love seat, chair and table set. It was loaded with a miniature refrigerator, microwave and a private bath.

A pretty good setup when you pimpin' Uncle Sam for the rent. I went over to answer the door and it was Cory.

"Whaddup playa," he asked, strolling inside. He was dressed down in a hunter green and white snap on Nike sweat suit and a pair of white Nike's he'd bought earlier at the mall.

Cory is about 6'4, 235 pounds, thick and muscular. He wears a low cut fade, with boss ass waves and has a hairless babyface. The ladies are definitely known to fall at his feet but not tonight. Tonight was my night to shine with babygirl.

Cory jumped in his low rider and I jumped into my gold '98 Hyundai Elauntra, and headed down Jackson Street.

The parking lot of the NCO club was as packed as the inside. Wall-to-wall and curb-to-curb honies. All shapes, sizes and colors. I mean, so many honeys that if you blinked, you missed three or four walk by. They were out in full effect. I'd bet my pay check, 99% was some poor dumb soldier's wife. She at the club, spending all his money, looking flossy and about to be somebody's boy toy for the night. His ass is out in the field on some training exercise, eating powdered processed food. Marriage, for that reason alone, definitely was not an option for me. Not in Uncle Sam's house.

The NCO club was off the chain. We found a table near the dance floor but far back enough to be comfortable and out of the flow of the crowd. The ladies wasted no time prancing over to introduce themselves. Cory was in "hoochie heaven." I was looking for baby girl but I couldn't find her. I bought me a Sex on the Beach and chased it with a Coors Light. After about an hour, I started to feel a little stood up, but you know a nigga like me is too cool to admit he got played. So the next honey that asked me to dance, I accepted. When I turned towards the bar I was on the dance floor groovin' with a Jamaican honey and there Alicia was. Standing on the corner of the first step, watching me.

I stopped dancing and quickly apologized to the female I was with and went towards her. She was dressed to kill. She had on a black full-figured body suit, with a long sleeveless jacket. I looked her up and down, taking in every inch of her. From her beautiful wavy hair, which was pulled back into a ponytail, to her pretty painted toes with gold rings, in her black sandals. Before I reached her, she had already turned down three brothers to dance. I smiled and asked, "Should I be afraid to ask you to dance with me?"

"Never that," she said as she took my hand. "Let's do it."

We walked to the middle of the floor and got our groove on to some reggae music. She moved to the rhythm like a Jamaican angel. A few songs later, a slow jam by Joe bumped out over the speakers. I grabbed her close to me, hoping she wouldn't feel the hardness of my jimmy that sprang up from watching her dance. Her body was so soft. The music was pumpin'. "...I'll touch all the places he would not and some you never knew would get you hot..."

Alicia smelled of Channel No.5. The touch of her hands on my back was exciting me. She whispered in my ear. "So, where's your other half tonight? Is she at home, thinking you're out with the fellas, or is she laid back in lingerie, waiting for you? Oh, I'm sorry. Playa's don't have just one woman."

"Playa? Why I gotta be all that?"

"They say dogs travel in packs, and I know your boy over there is definitely bow wow material.."

"True dat, I'ma let you have that one. But, they also say opposites attract. We down like fo' flat tizes, but I don't roll like that."

"So, if you don't roll like that, then why don't you have a woman?"

"I haven't found the right shorty yet. With me being in the army I'm gone alot and some women just can't handle that. I mean just look around you. I'd be pissed if I was in the field swattin' mosquito's and smellin' funky armpits and my woman was all up in here grindin' on some nigga. Can't do it, so I'm solo."

"What a shame," she said with a devilish grin. This girl was all that.

Just as I was getting into the groove, I felt a tap on my shoulder. I turned to see Cory gesturing to cut in. I started to snap but instead I bowed down. I didn't want her to think I was trippin' or that I was the jealous type.

Instead, I went back to the table and ordered another drink. I tried not to look at them, but I couldn't help it. I knew Cory. If she gave him an inch, he'd take a mile. I just kept thinking to myself, damn, I'll be glad as hell when this song is over.

Just my luck, they stayed on the floor for three more songs. While I was watching the action, a gorgeous young lady came over to talk to me. Light skinned with short hair dyed burgundy in a Halle Berry style cut. I was about to ignore her, fine-ness and all, until I got a full scope of her. Instead, I told her to have a seat. She glided down into the chair with a gentle ease and sat down her drink.

"So, what's your name?" she asked.

"Arman', yours?"

"Terri." She extended her hand to me. I welcomed it in mine. It was soft like silk. "So, how old are you Ms., or is it Mrs. Terri?"

"Miss. I'm twenty, first year in the army. I'm a finance officer for Pac, 1st maintenance Co. You?"

"Twenty four, 25th Infantry Division. My first year also. You live here on base?"

"Jefferson Court Barracks, you?"

"Hull St. Barracks."

She scooted closer for me to inhale her Cool Water perfume.

"You are very handsome Mr. Arman', you here alone?" When she asked that, I glanced up at the dance floor to see Alicia and Cory still partying.

I turned to her and said, "Looks that way."

"In that case, dance with me."

She grabbed me by the hand and led me to the middle of the dance floor. I backed off and watched Terri dance. I could tell she worked out by the way her legs looked in her burgundy and white tennis skirt. She was dancing like she was performing for me. She would put a hump in her back and grind up on me. Raise

6

her legs around my waist and throw it at me. She would turn her body in a way where her skirt would fly up and show me the black lace panties she wore underneath.

When the music slowed down, she grabbed me and pulled me close to her. I smelled her hair, perfume and sweat. I asked her, "So, are you here alone Miss Terri?"

"Yep. Tryin' to get over a love gone bad. Tryin' to see if I'm still attractive to the fellas. They way I see it, if I got someone as fine as you are to dance with me, then I must be doin' pretty good, wouldn't you say?"

"I'd say you're crazy for ever doubting yourself. You're gorgeous. A lil wild maybe, but definitely gorgeous."

"Wild huh? Tame me then."

I raised an eyebrow. "Depends on what you mean by tame."

She smiled and said, "All I need is a little attention, a little lovin' and I'll be mellow."

It hit me then, for about fifteen minutes or so, I hadn't thought about Cory or Alicia. I was engulfed in Terri. I looked to the table and they were handing each other small white pieces of paper. I assumed they were exchanging numbers. It stung a little bit, but oh well, bump it. I let it be. Terri pinched me and said, "Hello, are you there?"

"I'm sorry baby...why don't we get together and go to the show or something? Leave me your number and I'll hit you tomorrow about seven thirty."

"Ok."

We walked back towards the table and Alicia and Cory were gone. I was in a wish-wash wave of emotions. Part of me said forget it and the other half wanted to know what they were doing. The curious half won the battle. "Excuse me baby girl for one second. I'll be right back."

I walked throughout the club, trying to spot them and I couldn't find them anywhere. Knowing Cory, they were probably outside in the jeep freakin'. But, I couldn't really get with that cause Alicia didn't come across to me as that sorta chick. I can't believe she played me like that. Especially after all that bullshit

7

flirting. I looked back over to the table and noticed Terri was about to leave. I sprinted back across the club and caught her just in time.

"Hey boo, where you off too?" I asked.

"I thought you forgot about me, so I was heading out."

"I apologize. I saw someone I knew and got to talkin'."

"She must've been awful cute."

"Naw baby, nothing like that. So let me get your number so we can hook up tomorrow."

We exchanged numbers and I asked if she wanted an to escort to her car. She replied that she was waiting on her girlfriend to come out the restroom and she'd be fine. I kissed her on the cheek and said, "Be safe baby. I'll get in touch with you as soon as I finish my runnin' around tomorrow."

I headed for the door thinking I was so glad I drove my own damn car. This was not the first time Cory left me at the club to go freak with some chick. On the way home, all I thought about was how could she play me like that.

The next day, I refused to go to the PX. I couldn't stand to even look Alicia in the face. I avoided Cory as well. I knew he just wanted to bragg about the shit, so I said the hell with him for the day also. I pretty much laid back; chilled and watched Shaq and Kobe demolish the Trailblazers.

At seven, I hit Terri on her pager and she immediately called me back.

"Who you?" I asked, as if I didn't know.

"Hey tiger, it's me, Terri. What's up?"

"Not too much besides you baby. You still wanna catch a movie?"

"You know it. I even got my hair and nails done for this special occasion."

"Is that right? So you'll be ready in an hour or so?"

"Yep."

"Aight, I'll call you and get the room number."

"Ok."

CHAPTER 2

I jumped in the shower and put on a Phem short set. Spruced on some CK1 and bounced. On the way, I stopped by the Class Six to pick up a pack of gum. Brotha's breath had to be straight. When I arrived and Terri opened the door, I almost exploded on sight. She wore a black see through dress, no bra. I could see her pretty round nipples saying hello to me. Her dress ended right above the crotch area and her hair was hooked. She extended her hand and I noticed her middle finger nail had my name on it. I smiled to myself...flossy.

She invited me inside. Her room was the exact duplicate of mine except her furniture was black. I noticed two Blockbuster movies on the table.

"We still going out?" I asked.

"Sorta. I thought you might like a private showing so I went out and picked up a couple. I hope you don't mind."

"Naw, it's cool with me. Whatever you want."

"Now now, be careful what you say to me. I just might hold you to that."

"You do that," I chuckled.

Terri led me over to the love seat and offered me a drink. I took a Seagram's Seven and Coke. She popped in Rush Hour and came to sit beside me. She snuggled up under my arm, and a brotha was glad he used deodorant. Getting more comfortable, she gently laid her head upon my chest. About half way through Chris Tucker trying to teach Jackie Chan how to put some soul in the word ya'll, Terri rose up and smiled at me.

"You know you have very beautiful eyes. I wonder if I stare into them long enough could I see your heart."

"I don't know, why don't you try?"

She propped herself upon the love seat and pierced into my eyes. Moments later, she leaned in to kiss me. First my cheeks and then my forehead. She then started to kiss my neck and I got a hard on, again. She looked at me and asked, "When is the last time a woman's kissed you right?"

"I don't know. Depends on what you call right."

"Let me show you."

Terri started kissing my lips, softly and gently. Slowly, she nibbled on my bottom lip and then took her tongue and traced the outer rim of my mouth. Her tongue was very warm and soft. I opened my mouth to receive it and she backed away. Then she rushed my mouth and swallowed me completely. The feel of her mouth, the smell of her perfume, along with the Seagram's Seven was getting too much for me.

I placed my hands on her face. I ran my fingers from behind her neck down to her lower back. She responded with the same. I put her on top of my lap in a straddling position. Her dress rose up and I gripped her soft and thick thighs. I squeezed them harder with each stroke, letting her know how good they felt to me. I brought my hands with a force around her ass and underneath her thong. I could feel the heat from her oven baking the juices of love inside her. She was soaking wet. I thrust my finger inside her continuously and viciously. Her moans became more intense and She was all over my neck and chest. My shirt was off and she was unbuttoning my jeans. She climbed off my lap and stood in front of me.

Terri let her dress fall to the floor and she stood there naked in her black leather pumps. Her body glowing in beauty. She turned off the TV and flipped on the stereo. The sounds of Luther Vandross filled the room. ".....it would be so nice, if only for one night...."

This was trippin' me out. Usually, it's the man who know the quickest way to get a woman out of her panties is to throw on some Luther. Terri was seducing me and it was all good. She reached for my hand and stood me up. She bent down to untie my Nike's.

"You don't have to do that, I'll get it," I said.

"That's okay. Tonight, I'll do everything for you. It's all about you tonight. I'm here to please you so, just kick back and relax." She walked to my backside. "Your back is so tense; maybe you should lie down and let me massage it for you."

She took her tongue and began going up and down the middle of my back.

"Do whatever you wanna do baby."

"Now I told you to be careful what you say to me."

"Go for what you know."

Terri laid me down in the middle of her black lacquer bed and pulled out the baby oil. "I'll be right back."

She returned with warm baby oil and grapes. She placed the grapes on the night stand and poured the oil in her hands. She rubbed her hands together as she came to the bed and straddled my back. The oil felt so good upon my skin. She massaged my back, arms, legs and feet. She definitely knew how to make a man feel good. Getting more into it, she rolled me onto my back and massaged my chest. She proceeded to feed me grapes as the song, "Always and Forever," bumped over the airwaves.

Terri began to kiss my eyes, my lips, and my neck before moving down to my chest. She licked across my nipples with a craving for them. She glided her tongue across my stomach and she went down to my feet and placed each toe in her mouth. Lord have mercy, what a feeling! I had never felt nothing like it before. Her tongue moved up the back of my leg and kissed the back of my knees. Major sensitive spot that made my body jerk. Terri was pleased by my reaction as she picked up jimmy and placed it between her breasts. With the oil from my massage as lubrication, she moved up and down and almost brought me to a climax but wanting the moment to last, I held fast. When she saw what she was doing to me, she smiled and said, "What's your fantasy? It's all about you tonight."

"You seem to have it all under control. Don't stop, everything you do to me feels good."

"Really, watch me make it feel better."

She placed her tongue at the bottom of my jimmy and ran it up the back and down the front. She then wrapped her lips around to the top of it, and with a strong sucking motion, went down on it.

The force of her mouth drove me crazy. She went down with a soft gentle touch and then come back up with a force that left me damn near breathless. I moaned out her name. "Oohh Terri...that feels so damn good, baby. Get it all, baby, show me how much you can take."

Terri came up to the top again, and with one swoop, took down my entire jimmy into her mouth. I could feel the head poking the back of her throat. But, not once did she gag! She was making good love to it and I begged her to stop so I could go inside her of course but she wouldn't hear of it. She kept going until I couldn't take it any longer.

"I'm cumin' baby, take it out, hurry before..."

I felt it build up to the tip of my jimmy. I reached to take it out of her mouth but she pushed my hand. Then with a powerful suck, she made me cum so hard, I screamed like a lil bitch. As my nut pumped out into her throat, she sucked harder. Finally she let it go, but only to swallow. SWALLOW!! Then she got back on it to make sure she got everything. I couldn't stop trembling and my jimmy wouldn't go soft. She began to kiss my chest again. Then she looked at me licking her lips.

"UMMM, delicious. Tell me...did I please you?"

Before I could answer, she kissed me hard on the mouth. The thought of me nutting inside her mouth moments before took the kiss to a whole new level. I tried to switch positions and climb on top...she wasn't having it. She rose up, looked me in the eyes, reached for the baby oil and poured it down her chest. Seconds later, she grabbed my jimmy and teasingly put it inside her. She reached in the nightstand and pulled out a condom. I laughed and said, "Damn, you were really prepared for this, huh?"

"You bet yo' ass I was."

She climbed back on top of my jimmy and pushed the head inside of her. Surprisingly, she was tight. It took a minute for me to get all the way inside her. But once I did, the combination of the warmth of her walls, the hotness of her juices and the heat generating from the oil on our bodies, drove me crazy.

Her body took complete control as she rode me like a pure stallion. You feel me? She controlled the muscles inside her womb that made her grasp my jimmy tighter and tighter. She took her hands off the bed, placed them on my hips and began sexing me at a pace my wildest dreams couldn't take me. Faster and faster, tighter and tighter, she went until I grabbed both sides of the bed and screamed her name, "Oh Terri...Terri...I..I can't take no more...ooooohhhhh...ooooohh stop baby...please...Terri..."

She kept going until she felt me about to explode. She yelled, "Cum with me baby...cum with me...ooohhh, it feels so big...let me have it...let me feel all of it...let me feel it...tell me its mine..."

"Oh it's yours baby girl...all yours...OOOOHHHHH...." I gripped her ass as tight as I could, and she pulled me to her and locked her legs behind my back. She grabbed me around my neck, and at the same time we came long and we came hard. We both screamed out in passion. Our hearts beat a mile a minute until we couldn't take it anymore. We collapsed and once I caught my breath, I asked, "Where on earth did you learn to rock like that at age twenty?"

"I told you, I'm in the habit of pleasing. Are you pleased?"

"For the record, I'm whipped."

We both started laughing but I was serious. Never had I felt so good sexually in the company of a woman. I held her tightly to my chest. I'm so glad you came by tonight Arman'. I hope this won't be the last time I get the pleasure to be with you."

"I'm not like that Terri, I don't roll like that. As often as you want to see me, I'm here." With that she drifted off to sleep in my arms. I no longer cared about Alicia getting with Cory. This here was alright with me.

The next morning, we went to Denny's for breakfast. Afterwards, I drove Terri back to the room and kissed her goodbye.

"You want to call you later," she asked.

"You'd better, cause you'll be on my mind all damn day. If I'm not in my room, hit me on my hip."

13

When I left her, I went to my room to shower and change. I picked up my pager off the dresser and glanced through the numbers. Cory had called a couple of times. I left my pager at the room on purpose. I guess the deal with Alicia bothered me more than I cared to admit. That was last night though, before Terri introduced me to her world of sexual pleasure. I lay there on my bed thinking about the night before until I was about to flip. I had to do something.

I went outside to wash my car. I had taken out all the mats and vacuumed the inside before I realized that I had no Armor-All. When it came to washing my ride this was a necessity. The closet place to get some...the PX.

Maybe she ain't there, I reasoned. No such luck. When I walked inside, there she was, running the express lane. I had only one item, and if I had gone to another counter to check out, she would've known I was tripping about the way she played me. I couldn't give her that satisfaction. I strolled through her line, trying to appear cool. As usual, she smiled and greeted me, which made it harder to be upset.

"Have fun the other night," she asked.

"It was aight. I see you enjoyed yourself so much you cut out early huh?"

"My friends anted to go to the Embassy. And besides, you couldn't have enjoyed my company to tough?"

"Why do say that?"

"Because I haven't heard from you."

"Heard from me? How were you supposed to hear from me?" I smelled game in the air. "You didn't even say goodbye to me and you damn sho' didn't leave me no number. Besides, you seemed occupied."

"Occupied, with who?"

"My boy."

"Please, that fool. I told you he wasn't about nothing at the mall that day. Is that why you haven't called me?"

My voice rose slightly as I asked how the hell I was supposed to call her without a damn phone number. She put her hand up to silence me. "Wait a minute; I go on break in five minutes. Can you wait on me outside?"

I waited outside by my car until she came out a few minutes later. She was in a pair of blue jeans bib shorts, looking good as always. When she reached me, she stopped and threw her hand on her hip. I responded by throwing my hands in the air in surrender and said, "So what's up with this stuff about me not calling you?"

"I gave Cory my number to give to you. He gave me your room number and pager number but I didn't want to call you until called me first."

"What?" I thought back to the sight of them exchanging numbers at the table. Damn, so it was all about me.

"My bad, sweetheart. I thought you were tryin' to hook up with my boy so I backed off."

"Ain't no way…I told you Cory is too played out for me. Besides, I left and didn't say goodbye cause you was on the dance floor getting yo' freak on. Since I had to go, I told him to hook that up. I can't believe he didn't tell you. Well, actually I can."

"Well, he paged me a couple of times yesterday. I was runnin', though. I'm sure that's what he wanted but I didn't get a chance to get back at him."

Alicia leaned against my ride, smiled and grabbed my hand. "So, now that all that's straightened out, when am I gonna hear from you?"

"Page me and put your number in. I'm about to go and finish washing my ride and I'll hit you back later."

"Aight now, don't keep me waiting another two days. You know what they say, wait long, wait wrong."

"I heard that baby, check you out."

She opened my car door and I got inside. She leaned inside and kissed me on the cheek. "Drive carefully, wouldn't want you to hurt that handsome face."

As I pulled off, we waved to each other. I was basking in the game. Damn, I got her after all.

15

Then, I thought of Terri. Shit, she was expecting me tonight and I was really digging her. I'd just tell her I got caught up in a prior engagement. I couldn't leave her alone just yet. Especially when I didn't know what was up with ol' girl yet.

I went back to the room and called Terri. Her sexy voice came over the receiver. "Hello"

"Hey you, what you up to?"

"Missin' you," she said in a sweet voice.

"You're about to be mad at me." I paused. "I can't make it tonight. I totally forgot I had prior plans to hook up with my boy Cory. He just called. I'm sorry boo but I promised him." I waited for a response. "You mad at me?"

"Of course not, boo, handle yo' business and make sure you call me when you get in. Time is not an issue. I'll be waiting."

"Are you this sweet to everybody or just me?"

"Just you, Swack!" She blew me a kiss and hung up the phone. She was all right. Some women get silly when they don't get what they want. But she was cool about the situation. Now I had to concentrate on Alicia.

CHAPTER 3

"......can't deny me, why would you want to, you need me. Why don't you try me, baby you'd want to believe me..." Jay-Z was pumping, as I put the finishing touch on my ride.

That afternoon, I chose some of my flyest Polo gear to sport. I got all dabbed up while jamming Mystikal on the stereo. When I finished, I called up my favorite cashier.

"Hello," a female voice answered.

"Hello, may I speak to Alicia?"

"This is she."

"Hey, how you feel about catchin' a movie tonight?"

"I'm down for whatever. Give me a minute to take care of a few things and I'll be finished about eight thirty, okay?"

It was only six thirty so that left me three hours to kill. I decided to pop over Terri's to see what she was into.

"Hey baby, it's good to see you," she said as she jumped into my arms.

"Now that's the kind of welcome a nigga wanna come home to after a hard days work."

"I thought you were hooking up with yo' boy?"

"We are. He just had something else to do first so I ended up with a couple of free hours. What better way to kill time than to spend it with you. But now...if you want me to leave.."

"Try it if you want to and I'll tie yo' fine ass to that bed over there," she said laughing.

"Shit, that'll work"

"Come on in and sit down."

I walked over to her love seat, sat down and thought back to the night before. I looked at her and smiled because she was so damn sexy. She had a pan of soapy water on the floor in front of her chair and a similar one on the table beside her.

"I was just about to begin my pamper day. You know, my feet, a facial, and things like that."

"What? Ching Chang ain't poppin' no more?"

17

She laughed and threw a towel at me.

"Hell, I thought all ya'll went to them Chinese folks."

"For my nails maybe, if I want something special. Other than that, I take care of myself. Try to keep myself beautiful."

"And that you are."

She smiled and I sat there watching her. We talked about a lot of things as she soaked, scrubbed, cut and filed her toenails. She then oiled and painted them. She really did have nice feet. And that's a good thang cause don't no man want to look down the legs of a fine ass woman and see more corn than that on the cob. You know one of them women, fine from the ankles up.

Terri's legs were nice and cleanly shaved. She had on this skimpy pair of pink shorts. That had jimmy on hard as she sat there looking amazing.

We continued to talk about our jobs and the upcoming possibility of a war in Iraq.

"I hope you don't have to go. I would really miss you something awful," she said.

"You would, huh?"

She came over to me and kissed me very seductively. "You bet yo' ass I would." She placed her hands down my Polo sweats and pulled out my jimmy. Twirling and twisting it, she had me horny as hell and ready to roll. "Let me do you," she whispered.

"Do me baby."

Terri kneeled down and removed my shoes and socks. Then started rolling up the bottom of my sweats. I'm like, okay, this is some new shit. She left the room and returned with a pan of clean soapy water. She sat the pan down on the chair, kneeled in front of me and placed the towel from her shoulders onto the floor. She placed the pan beneath me and placed my feet inside. She noticed the look on my face and smiled.

"Where's your mind Arman?"

"Hell, you the one got a nigga all excited and shit, talkin' bout let me do you. I didn't know you was talkin' bout no feet."

"I wasn't."

She rose up to me and lay down across me on the couch, with her head in my lap. She picked up my jimmy and went to work. Slowly, at first, then with a monitored speed that took me away to another place. A place where sex like she dished out was forbidden. She came up slow and took it all the way to the back. She moved her muscles at the rear of her throat and massaged the tip of my jimmy. With my hands resting on her shoulders and my eyes closed, she jacked, sucked and jacked some more. Her lips felt so soft and warm.

"Gimme what I want," she demanded.

"Anything you want babygirl, it's yours. It's your world."

"I know." With that, she sucked powerfully and forcefully until she got it all. DAMN!!

Terri looked at me and smiled. "I think your feet are ready." I think I'm done, I said to myself resting my head on the back of the sofa. Terri was a master at pleasure. She scrubbed my feet, cut my nails, then oiled and massaged them.

Afterwards, she did my nails and put a coat of clear polish on top. She kissed me on the cheek.

" I'll be right back. I gotta run out to the car for a second while those dry."

It took her about twenty minutes to return and I had dozed off. She returned with an arm full of Long John Silvers'.

"Baby," I said, rising up to help her. My knees were still weak as hell. "You didn't have to go and get nothin' to eat."

"I know I didn't, but I couldn't have my man out there hungry now could I?"

"So I'm yo' man now," I asked while putting my hand underneath her shorts. "So this is mines right?"

"Every wall, every orgasm and every drop of juice."

When Alicia paged me, it was a quarter to eight. Terri was cuddled in my arms watching TV.

"Aw boo, that's my boy Cory," I said checking my two-way. "I gotta go."

She rose up and grabbed me by the hand. "Go on and have a good time. Call me later." Terri saw me to the door, kissed me and sent me on my way, no further discussion. Damn, if a nigga could clone that, I'd be a rich muthafucka.

CHAPTER 4

The movie Alicia and I chose was *Enemy of the State* with Will Smith. In the middle of the movie, my pager went off. It was Cory. I excused myself and went to the phone to call him back. I knew he was pissed cause I hadn't returned his calls.

"Talk to me," he answered.

"Whaddup Playa?"

"Nigga what, you don't know nobody no mo'?"

"It's blue nigga, you know it ain't like that dawg. I been trippin'. I got up with this honey at the club last night, you know, after yo' ass left me. You remember the honey with the tennis skirt on? Her."

"I heard that, but listen, I been callin' you cause babygirl from the exchange wanted me to give you her hookup. I started not to, but you know I don't cock block and I definitely ain't no hater."

"She with me now at the show. I caught up with her at the PX. You know playa, the real reason I didn't get back at you was cause I thought you hit it and was callin' to brag about the shit."

"Hol' up nigga, even if I did hit it, I know you wasn't bout to let no broad come between us? I know we better than that."

"My bad, playa. You know we down..."

"Like fo' flat tizes.you know it, so act it. Quit bitchin' up nigga." He paused and then said, "So you gon' hit that or what?"

"Damn, slow down boy. We only at the movies. I don't know what's up with her yet. But man; let me tell you about babygirl from the club. Dawg."

"She in there?"

"Like dat there, "I said as we both laughed.

"But let me get back inside, man, I'll holla at you later."

"Aight playa, stay up."

We hung up and I went back inside. I returned with popcorn and soda. I only bought one because it cost too damn much but I told Alicia it was more romantic to just share one. Smooth, huh?

When we left the movies, I took Alicia to Red Lobster to eat. She insisted on paying her way. At first it sorta bothered me but then I figured, what the hell? If she wanna pay, let her pay. I fed her crab from my fingers and she complimented me on my nicely manicured hands. "Nice to see a brotha take care of himself." I smiled and thought of Terri.

After we ate…well, she ate, because I was still full from the Long John's, we went to the Landing to talk. One of the prettiest sights in Texas is the Landing by the river. The lights lit up the water and the horse drawn carriages gave it a romantic appeal. Hand in hand we strolled.

"So, tell me again why you're not with anyone," I asked.

She hesitated for a moment and then spoke softly. "Well, I was in love with a guy a few years back. You know, the whole high school sweetheart thing. He wanted to marry me, so he said. He was stationed here while I attended college back home in Austin. I came here to live with him, and when I arrived, I found some things that didn't quite sit right with me."

"He was playin' you?"

"To say the least. So, we tried to work it out but I knew I deserved better and he deserved worse. Either way, I left him and had my sister Punkin move up here with me. He went on to Fort Polk, LA and I got a job at the PX. Now, enough about me, what about you?"

"I've had my share of broken hearts. My first one was by my third grade teacher," I said, smiling. "Naw, seriously though, I'm that nice guy that girls always seem to take as being weak because I like to spoil'em and threat them nice. My moms taught me how to respect women and treat them how I would want a man to treat her or my sisters. But like I said, some females take kindness for weakness. So, I decided to chill and let cupid shoot his arrow in my ass for a change." We went on at this pace for what seemed like hours.

When I drove Alicia home and walked her to the door, she turned to me and smiled.

"I had a really good time tonight. I hope I hear from you soon."

"I had a good time too. You're a beautiful lady, inside and out. When I get in, I'll call and let you know I made it home safely."

"You do that." She turned to walk away and then turned back. Alicia kissed me softly on the cheek. "Weak is the last word I'd use to describe you."

I smiled.

"Drive carefully," she said.

I walked away thinking to myself, she too, would have to stick around for a while.

At two in the morning, my pager went off and it was Terri. I had forgotten to call her. As I drove home, I kept telling myself not to get into something I couldn't get myself out of. I liked both Terri and Alicia.

When I got in, I returned her page.

"Hey you," she answered.

"How did you know it was me?"

"Cause…when the phone rung, I got all moist between the legs."

"Straight?"

"That, plus I got Caller ID."

"Oh, I see you got jokes, huh?" What you doin'?"

"Missing you. I just called to see if you had a good time tonight with your boy. I've been thinking about you since you left. It's really got me trippin' how we click together, boo."

"Yeah I feel you. The entire time I was with my boy tonight, I was thinking bout you. Thinking bout how good you make me feel."

"Really?"

"No doubt."

"That's so sweet. Will I see you tomorrow?"

"It depends on how late we have to work. We're preparing for section evaluations next week so I might get off late this entire week. I don't wanna bug you too late."

"When it comes to you, time is not an issue. I don't care if you get off at three in the morning; you can pop over whenever cause you got it like that. Call me tomorrow before you leave for work, ok?"

"Aight, then, got it like that. I'll hit you in the morning. Later sweetheart, goodnight."

I hung up the phone and called Alicia.

"Hey, did I wake you," I asked.

"Naw its okay. I wasn't out yet. Glad you made it home in one piece."

"Shit, me too. So why you still up? Can't sleep; got a nigga on yo' mind, huh?"

"Yeah right, you wish."

We laughed.

"No, I'm just trying to finish up reading one of my romance novels. Something I enjoy very much."

"Aw yeah, so does that mean I can look forward to lots of little romantic surprises?"

"It depends."

"On?"

"On how good you act. You might get lots of romantic surprises."

"Is that right?"

"That's right," she said.

"And for your first one, I want to cook you dinner tomorrow night. What's your favorite?"

"Without a doubt, collard greens, Mac & cheese, catfish, chitlins and sweet potato pie."

"A soul food man, huh? Aight, I'll see what I can work out. I might be able to do a lil somethin' somethin'. So how about eight?"

"We'd better make it nine. We got evals next week and I might get off late. But if that's too late, we can make it another day."

"Naw, nine's cool. I'll call you around seven to make sure you can still make it." she said.

"Aight baby, I'll holla at you then, sweet dreams."

I lay back on my pillow and thought back over the last twenty-four. It had been filled with all kinds of different emotions. Passion, jealousy, anger, lust and excitement. Each woman had different qualities I was attracted to.

Terri was exciting, sexy and freakish...oh so freakish. She was every man's fantasy in the bedroom. A spur of the moment type honey. And that body...DAMN!

Alicia is more of a good conversationalist. She's more laid back, sorta homey like. The kind you take home to your mother. She reads romance novels and shit like that. Normally, this wouldn't have been an issue but it seemed as if I was falling for both too hard and way too fast.

In a dilemma, I decided to call and talk to the "mack" himself about the situation. The phone rung about four times before he answered, sounding all out of breath.

"Who dis," he asked?

"It's me balla, whaddup? Damn nigga, you hittin' skins at three in the morning?"

"Fo' sho....oohhh yeah babygirl, right there, yeah right there....so...what's up man, you get that?"

"Naw, man, I didn't try to. Shit, sound like you getting' enough for the both of us. And after Terri, babygirl from the club, I probably couldn't get it up anyway. I need to holla at you later on. When you get done, get at me."

"Hol' up, this sounds serious. Hol' up baby, my boy needs to holla at me..."

"But, Cory baby, I wanna have some fun. Can't he call back," I heard her say.

"...Look, you give good hummer and all, but don't overstep yo' talent. I said my boy need to holla at me, just chill fo' a minute aight? Aight playa, holla at yo' boy."

I lay back and tripped off how Cory handled his women, or more so, how they let him get away with it. I chuckled and said, "Man, she sounds a lil needy right now. Maybe you should handle that and then get at me."

"Man she'll be aight. Chickens come a dime-a-dozen. We boyz fo' life. Down...."

"Like fo' flat tizes," we said together. "Holla at me."

"Well, it's like this...you know the honey I keep tellin' you about?"

"Yeah, yeah, the one with the booty fo' days, what about her?"

"We suppose to hook up to go to the movies right, but when I get to her barracks to..."

"She AD(active duty)?"

"Yeah, man, anyway, she rented Rush Hour and we chilled in. Then baby girl got at me and started kissin' on a nigga. She massaged me with hot baby oil, fed me grapes, gave a nigga a manicure, pedicure and...C, man she gave me two hummer jobs straight outta porn 2000, you hear me? She swallowed, man..."

"What?"

"Yess....nigga nutt and all!"

"Damn, you a lucky mothafucka," he said.

"Then she got down on it and rode me like a stallion. I mean this gal was on and poppin'. And she don't miss a beat. She even had her own supply of Trojans."

"Aight nigga, you know what they say about them ho's that carry they own, they some dick happy ho's," he laughed.

"Naw, man, she ain't like that. She cool people. The kinda honey a nigga just wanna hang out with all the time. Now Alicia, she's more of the quiet type. Reads romance novels and shit."

"Aw, hell naw. Now, you know women that like them novels and soap opera's and shit are all dramatic and shit. All of them wanna be actresses and expect you to be like them corny mothafucka's in them books." The chick in the background said, "That's not true Cory, we just like men to pay us some attention"

"You want some attention? Here....anyway man...uummm...so...uuummmm...what you gon' do.....ooohh yeeaahh...about this shit?" It was obvious that ole girl was back on the job again. I'd let Cory handle his business and get back at me later. Shit, we had to be at PT(physical training) in three hours.

"I don't know man," I said.

"Chill with both of 'em until I know which one I definitely wanna kick it with. But right now, nigga, I gots to go cause ya'll makin' me sex sick. I'll holla playa."

"Aight playa, I'll see you at...OW! DAMN! Watch the teeth! Let me go fo' I have to hurt this damn gal."

"See you at work."

As he hung up the phone, I heard him say to her, "Damn baby, if you needed instructions on how to give a hummer job, you shoulda asked." Then the line went dead.

When it came to women, me and Cory was so damn different. I would never treat a woman the way he does. Objects, toys...never the beautiful flowers they are. To me, a woman's attitude makes her either ugly or beautiful. Some of the most unsightly women are made lovely because their attitudes make them that way. You ever see a fine ass woman walking down the street with a tore-up from the floor-up brother and wonder how he pulled her? That's how.

To me, it makes no sense, spending all that time and money being beautiful on the outside and ugly on the inside. Why not just be ugly all around?

Anyway, I looked at the clock on the nightstand. It read 3:26am. I wondered was Terri still awake. I dialed her number and she answered in the sexiest whisper I'd ever heard.

"It's late Pam, what's up?"

"It's not Pam baby, it's Arman'. Did I wake you? I was thinkin' bout you and I couldn't wait until morning to hear your voice," I said.

27

"That's funny, baby, cause Luther's on the stereo and I was dreamin' about you too."

"Really now, and what were you dreaming?"

"How good your chest feels, how good you tasted, smelled and felt inside of me. How my body responded to the way you laid it down. Ohhh, its jerkin' now."

"Aight now, behave yo'self. I was wondering, and if I'm getting to deep off in yo' business, let me know. At the club, you said you were getting' over a love gone bad, what happened? I mean, who was the fool that let you get away?"

"Actually, boo; it was a marriage that went sour. When I was sixteen, I got involved with one of my brother's Army buddies and married him when I was eighteen. He was thirty and a Staff Sargeant. He had been in about twelve years at the time. A member of some of the Army's finest clubs. Top notch, soldier, and terrible husband. He wanted me to be like the white officer's wives. Knitting', swapping recipes, attending uppity functions with fake ass women, wearing fake ass smiles. He tried to mold me into the perfect military wife and that just ain't me. I can't be controlled. So, I divorced him, joined the best of the best and here I am. All wasn't lost though, I mean, he did teach me a lot about how a man likes to be treated. He taught me everything I know about sex. I think he did a pretty good job, don't you?"

"Aey, I gotta give him his props. He raised one hell-of-a-woman. So, tell me...what are you wearin'?"

We burst out laughing.

CHAPTER 5

At work the next day, all I could do was think about Terri. I was screwing up all the tests we were running on our guns. She had me caught up, plain and simple. Cory walked up to me at lunch time and said, "Damn man, whats up? You been lost all mornin'. Them broads got you trippin' fo' sho."

"Man, I'm supposed to hook up with both of 'em tonight. I wanna see Terri, but I know we just gon' end up fuckin' so I think I'll cancel."

"Hell naw..."

"Hell yeah. I'm telling you dawg, she somethin' else. But I need to see whats up with Alicia. She supposed to cook a nigga dinner. I'm a call Terri and tell her I'm working late. That way if things don't pop off with Alicia, I can still creep."

He gave me dap along with his pimp smile. "Sounds like a plan to me. I taught you well playa. Come on lets hit Mickey Dee's," he said slapping me on the back.

We took Cory's jeep and hit the highway. He popped in some Next and their song "Butta Luv" pumped put over his Kenwood's. "You got the love that I want; you got the love that I need..."

Yeah, I was tripping and I needed to get this deal with Terri and Alicia into perspective. I figured a dinner with Alicia was just what I needed.

While Cory went inside to get something to eat, I called Alicia at work.

"Just wanted to see if you still wanted some company tonite?"

"As a matter of fact, I'm writing down everything I'll need as we speak. I'll be waiting at nine."

"Should I bring anything?"

"Just you."

I hung up and dialed Terri on her cell. When she answered, I heard the sounds of Dru Hill in the background.

"Talk to me," she whispered.

"Damn you sound sexy, where are you?"

"On my way home to soak. We called it quits early today."

"Yeah soak them feet baby cause you been runnin' through my mind all day."

We laughed.

"Will I see you tonight," she asked.

"Sorry boo, not tonight. Gotta work late and believe me, I'm heart broken about it. But I promise, I'll get up with you tomorrow. Forgive me?"

"It's not your fault baby, of course I forgive you. Handle up and call me if you have time, ok?"

"You got it, baby. Be careful, I don't want a single scratch on that body and think of me," I said as suave as I could.

"No doubt boo."

Cory dropped me off at my ride to head home and prepare for my date with Alicia. I showered and dressed in a Hilfiger short set, freshly starched from the cleaners. I put on some Jon B to mellow me out as I brushed my waves and relined my goatee. I chose Eternity as my seduction scent that night.

When I arrived at Alicia's she was wearing a pair of jeans and a Kobe Bryant jersey. She made it look so damn good. She was flossy. As she led me to the living room, I watched her walk. The sway of her hips made me tingle. I wondered what they felt like.

I excused myself to check out her bathroom. My mother always told me, you can tell how clean a woman is and how she feels about herself by the way she keeps her bathroom. When I flicked on the light I was impressed. It was laid out in the colors of hunter green and champagne. I peeked behind the shower curtain and found a sparkling tub.

Under the sink, the cleaning supplies were nicely arranged and in the closet were organized hygiene products, including Summer Eve. I like...I definitely like.

For dinner, Alicia made corn bread, Mac & cheese, mustard greens (which I hate, especially out the can but I was polite and pretended there was no difference between them and collards. Every soul food eater knows there's a huge difference), catfish and pumpkin pie. Naw, no sweet potatoes and that would have been cool with me but the pie was store bought. Good thing she held a conversation better than she cooked.

We talked over dinner and afterwards I helped her wash the dishes. During this time, we talked some more about work and life.

"Well as I said, I was really in love with my high school sweetheart. I had saved all my money working my senior year to move up here to be with him. I decided to surprise him at our new apartment but when I arrived, some hoochie answered the door. The hoochie was half-naked, with weave hanging down her back, smiling from ear to ear. I dropped his ring at the door and left him there with his mouth hangin' open."

"Dammmnnnn!!

"I mean, we did try it again but it didn't work. Instead of leaving town, I moved in with my sister and started working. End of story. There's really not much to me. I like sports. As you can see I'm a Lakers fan and I love the Dallas Cowboys. I like to read and I like to go to the club and hang out with my friends every now and then. But I also like to snuggle up and stay at home. Your turn," she said as she placed a Miller Genuine Draft in front of me.

I smiled because that meant she really paid attention to what I bought when I came through her line at the PX. Again, I was impressed.

"Well, I'm from D-town, so no, I'm not too far away from home. Which means I'm a Cowboys fan also. Lakers are pretty tight, but I'm a Trailblazers fan."

She frowned, I smiled.

"I joined the military because I wanted to work and get a college fund. Plus stay off the streets, not to mention, Cory talked me into it. I'm gonna be an engineer. But right now I'm stuck in artillery. No kids, single and the only one I hang out with is Cory. He's like my brotha. We grew up in the same projects and I love

31

him to death, even if he is bow wow material." We playfully hit each other.

We went into the living room and sat on the couch. We continued to talk. I made no moves on Alicia and just enjoyed her conversation. I felt very at ease with her.

At the close of the evening, she walked me to the door and kissed me goodnight. I drove home to the sounds of Dru Hill. ".....these are the times we all wish for, the moment will last me so much more. We don't have to do a thang at all, we'll take our time and talk..."

As I hit the bed, I called Terri.

"So, what are you wearin'?"

"Shorts, u?"

"Absolutely nothing, I like to sleep free. I never know when I'll have an erotic dream or some strange man might break in and demand to screw me. I'd like to be ready," she said laughing.

"Aight, don't get nobody shot," I said, sharing her laughter.

"I feel you on sleepin' free, you know, walking around the crib butt naked sometimes. But unlike you, ain't no chance of no man runnin' up in here demandin' a damn thang."

We both laughed. She told me to tell her something good.

"I think you're an incredibly beautiful woman and a sex goddess."

"Why thank you, I think," she said giggling.

"I learn my body when I'm alone. In fact, the very thought of you started me to exploring. Like right now, I'm exploring my nipples with hot oil. OOOUUU, now I'm pourin' the oil on my stomach...its hot...I'm rubbin' it in now and my nipples have responded. They're burning in pleasure. My hand is now circling and massaging my thighs."

I moaned and said, "Touch 'em baby. Touch 'em for me."

"For you? For you, I'll touch more than that. For you, I'm touching my clit. Oh...its tingling baby..I'm pouring baby oil all over my mommy. Oooohhh baby...it feels so good. I'm rubbin' my lips with my fingers, wishing they were yours."

By now, I was stroking my jimmy up and down, imagining Terri rubbing her coochie.

"Put yo' fingers inside," I whispered.

"Tell me how it feels."

"It feels good daddy. You wanna hear how it sounds?"

After a short pause, the sounds of wet juices filled the telephone lines as she swished and swirled her fingers inside. It made a slight popping sound that drove me crazy.

I massaged my jimmy faster and faster, harder and harder. Terri's electrical partner clicked on and her moans became louder and more intense.

"Picture you, hittin' it from the back. I'm on all fours, spreaded wide for you. Face down, ass up. You're long strokin' it. Picture it daddy...picture it."

I did, and as I did, I began to talk to her more. "You like that?"

"Ooohhh, daddy...yes."

"Tell daddy if it feels good, baby."

"You know its da bomb, baby."

"I wanna hit harder, can I?"

"Like a mack truck. Ooohhh Arman'...I wanna cum but I want you to cum with me...will you baby? Will you cum with me?"

"Yeah babygirl...it about to explode for you. Come and get it baby...come and get it..."

I felt the sperm rise to the top. "I'm cummin'...oooohhh babyyyyy..."

As I heard her scream, I released all over my stomach and hand. She was in my ear panting. I tried to stop myself from shaking, more so, from the mental pleasure it gave than the physical.

"Nite."

Click...she hung up, just like that.

Damn, I was straight up in a daze. The girl made me buss one having phone sex. Never in my wildest dreams, and I've had some wild ones, would I have imagined a woman could have that kind of effect on me. Shit…this girl….I'd have to be out of my mind to stop seeing her..And I wasn't outta my mind by a long shot.

CHAPTER 6

For the next few months, thoughts of both Alicia and Terri filled my head and I continued to balance my time between the two of them. Terri continued to sex me up while Alicia and I grew closer mentally. Cory and I went to the club every now and then but I always found myself thinking about one or the other. At that point, I knew I was in to deep and before it got any deeper, I had to leave one alone. All night long, I weighed the options. Terri and I had nothing more than a sexual relationship. True, that was mostly my fault because she always wanted to spend time with me but I would always come up with an excuse to leave after all the lovemaking was over. And I wasn't sure I could give that up.

I was crazy about Alicia. She was everything a man could want in a sista. We hadn't had sex yet but that sorta kept me intrigued. She had mad respect for herself and I thought that was special. Not that Terri didn't, but what was between us besides sex? It took a couple of days but I finally decided it would be Terri I had to leave alone.

I called Terri and asked her to meet me down at the entrance of her barracks. I wanted to go for a ride and talk. When I pulled up, she had on a leather trench coat and black pumps looking fine as hell. The fact that it was hot outside and she was in a coat should've told me something was up. She climbed into the car and gave me a kiss.

"How was work boo? I've missed you the last couple of nights?"

"I'm sorry baby. Cory and I have been caught up working late."

"That's okay, I got you now. Let's go over to the park by the PX."

We pulled into the parking lot of the Long Branch Park. We walked over to the picnic bench and I sat down. I was wearing a pair of gym shorts and a t-shirt. Terri was standing in front of me, with her coat buttoned. I rubbed my hands down my thighs and took a deep breath.

"Terri, baby, we really need to talk. I know we been kickin' it for about six months or so but ..."

She walked towards me as if she could sense what I was about to say. She threw her arms around my neck and kissed my cheek. She whispered, "Shhh, don't say anything."

She took a few steps back and undid her coat. Wearing a black teddy, no panties and black garter belt, she let the coat fall to the ground. Afterwards, she took my hands and put them up to the straps of her lingerie. I pulled them off her shoulders and her breasts greeted me, seductively. They always had the power to hypnotize me.

Terri guided my hands to her breasts and with her hands on top of mine, she massaged them. I had to be real with myself; there would be no resisting her, not tonight. As she teased my lips with her tongue. I slid my hands around to her ass. She lifted my shirt and began to lick on my chest. Her bites were slow, gentle bites. Terri stuck her hand inside my shorts and pulled out my jimmy. I felt the heat of her tongue as it entered her mouth and she took it all the way back to her tonsils. Damn, she was good at that shit.

She lifted up and let my jimmy fall from her mouth. She lured me into a standing position, pulled down my shorts and boxers and spun me around until it was her who was near the table. Terri picked up her coat, laid in on the table and got into a doggy style position. I stopped using condoms months ago because I felt she was a cool person. More than anything, I felt safe with her.

Terri reached back, grabbed me by the jimmy and pulled me to her. She put her hand between her legs and spreaded her lips apart to receive me. I was a wanted guest. She was still tight as ever and so, so warm. The mommy was soak and wet and with every stroke became wetter and wetter. I moaned her name. She looked back at me and said, "Be still, don't move. Let me fuck you tonight."

She put a hump in her back and began to grind and roll all over my jimmy. It was like nothing I'd ever felt before. The more she threw her body, the closer she brought me to an eruption.

I guess she could feel me swelling because she snatched her body from mine, flipped around and with one swoop had me inside her mouth.

The wind began to blow a soft breeze against the wetness her mouth left on my jimmy as she went back and forth. She used both her mouth and her hands. When I was about to buss, she pulled back, gave me a funny look and in a soft, almost broken voice asked, "Arman' is sperm good for a baby?"

"Oh yeah, baby. It's...,BABY! What baby?"

I know she didn't just say baby. My jimmy immediately went limp. I slid out of her hand and stumbled backwards a step or two, jimmy hangin' and swangin'. I couldn't breathe. I pulled up my shorts and boxers. I walked back over to her.

"Come again...what baby?"

"The one I'm about to have with you. I've been waiting for the right time to tell you that you're gonna be a daddy. I'm six weeks along and you're the father."

My head was swirling and I damn near fell out.

"Damn Terri, I ain't tryin' to have no kids right now. I don't care if you had to send me a damn postcard, why didn't you say something? I looked at her, waiting for her usual chuckle that meant she was joking but nothing came.

"Terri that shit ain't funny. Are you fuckin' with me?"

She shook her head no. She appeared to be serious. I quickly became angry.

"I ain't got time for no....damn!"

My voice raised and she responded in the same manner.

"Look, it was your idea to stop using the damn rubbers! I wanna feel you skin-to-skin, boo. Ain't that what you said? I didn't plan for this to happen Arman'. I was on the pill. So don't stand there and treat me so damn cold!"

She was screaming at the top of her lungs while the tears streamed down her face.

I felt the same pain but I'm sure for different reasons. I know she wished I would have been happy about the news and my reaction hurt her deeply. I was more upset with myself for the stupidity of "skin-to-skin."

Yet with all my emotions, I had no right to blow up at her like I did. I walked over to comfort her. I pull her coat around her and brought her to my chest.

"I'm sorry, baby. I was caught off guard. I didn't mean to trip out on you. We're in this situation together."

I paused to gather myself. "So what do you want to do?"

"I really don't know, Arman'. Please, just give me some time to think about it," she said, as she wiped away her fallen tears. "Please don't hate me."

I kissed her forehead and told her I could never hate her and that everything would be all right. I didn't believe it but I said it.

When I dropped her off, I went straight over to Cory's room to holla at him about the shit I had gotten myself into.

"Whaddup playa," he said as he opened the door. I gave him some dap and sat down on the loveseat.

Cory's room was wall-2-wall Janet Jackson and Playboy centerfolds. On his bed was a Navy blue satin comforter with white designs of the sun, moon and stars. His ceiling was decorated with them as well, and when you turned off the lights, the decorations glowed in the dark. Cory always said it made him feel like he was fucking in space.

"Peep gam‚e playa, I done got myself into some shit. I went to break tf off with Terri cause I'm tryin' to be down with Alicia completely and Terri tells me she's pregnant."

"Aw shit, nigga! How the fuck did you let that shit happen? What the rubba popped?"

"Naw, man, I stopped using 'em months ago. I knew I was the only one hittin' it so, I said fuck'em. But dawg, I didn't think no shit like this was gon' happen."

"You damn right, yo' dumb ass didn't think. Nigga, condoms ain't just to keep you from getting' some skank pregnant.

Nigga, it's to protect yo' dick from all that incurable shit floatin' around out there. Damn, man, what the hell is wrong with you? Hol' up....I'm trippin'...I ain't gon' flip out...one question, when's the abortion?"

"I don't think..."

"What you mean you don't think? Not thinkin' is what got you into this shit from jump street. What's there to think about? I know you ain't finna sell out yo' life to some trick cause you think her pussy's like sunshine."

Cory handed me a glass of Alize' and sat next to me. "Dawg, are you sure she's pregnant? You know ho's be sayin' that shit sometimes tryin' to keep a nigga trapped. Take yo' ass to the clinic with her and see for yo'self. Then see how much it costs to get rid of it. Don't be no suck,a dawg."

"I know, man, I'm fresh outta b-camp and I don't need no shorty's right now..."

"Sure as hell don't," he added. "I'll see if we can swoop by the clinic tomorrow on our lunch breaks."

I picked up the phone and called Terri. I asked her if we could stop by Irwin Army on our breaks and she agreed. I picked her up, took her to eat, and headed for the clinic. We rode in silence most of the time, something very unusual for us. Normally we're talking shit and cracking jokes but not today. Today we had little to say.

I sat outside and I thought about Alicia. How could I expect to have a relationship with her if she finds out about Terri? Terri came out the clinic and handed me a pink slip of paper that read, "UGK: Positive."

I looked up at her and saw the tears flowing again.

"I'm sorry. I know you didn't want this but I'm not sure what I want to do just yet. I need some time. Time to think things through. Can you give me that?"

I felt as if my world was falling apart. Still I couldn't blame her. I sighed, "Well you know I go to the field on Monday and I'll be out there close to forty-five days. I mean, you can write to me and let me know what you decide. I'll try to have my phone on but the reception probably won't pick up."

I paused and tried to think of something else comforting to say but I couldn't.

"Well, I gotta get back to work. Come on, I'll drop you off. Don't worry aight? It's all good."

Terri grabbed me as I turned to walk away. "Arman' can't you at least tell me how you feel?"

I looked at the ground and softly replied, "I don't know."

I took her back to work, and as I headed for my quad, I contemplated the impact a shorty would have on my life. The bad points were I wasn't financially secure. Stable yeah, secure no. I wasn't in a stable position in the Army. My career was just beginning. I was gone a lot and had to be ready for war at any given moment. What kind of father could I be to my child, especially since I had no role model to follow?

I turned on the radio. Music always helped me think. "Just the Two of Us" by Will Smith came blaring through the speakers. "...I think to myself, damn, a little me..."

I visualized myself with a son, playing catch and talking about his girlfriends. My daughter, having me in her room for teatime and playing with her babydolls. Me, having to one day shoot some busta for hurting her. The thoughts made me both excited and afraid. I'd just have to think about it. Use the time in the field to sort it all out. After work, I told Cory about the test results. He shook his head and said, "Damn, dawg, she caught you trippin'. See you need to be like me. I don't let no ho catch me out there like that. So, what's up? She gon' get that done right?"

"She don't know, and actually, I don't know if I..."

"Aw shit, nigga, she got you trippin' fo' sho. What the hell you thinkin' about? Nigga, you barely making it by yo'self. You sending money home to handle yo' family and shit. How the hell you gon' take care of a shorty? Nigga, you crazy!"

"I'm sayin', though, man, if she have it, what I'ma do? Let my shorty grow up without me?"

"Hell yeah!"

"Man you out yo' damn mind. You forgot our punk ass daddy's weren't around and our moms had to struggle to keep shit together. Now, I'm not in love with Terri but I ain't gon' let my shorty suffer for that. You need to respect that. Yo' problem is you's a ho ass nigga. You dog women out. But that ain't me. I..."

"Nigga, I treat a woman by how she put herself out there. If she comes at me wrong, I'ma treat her wrong. They give up the pussy the first night and ask you, no, demand for you to respect them in the mornin'. I have yet to find a woman who had mad respect fo' themselves like Alicia do. Now how you gon' handle that?"

"I ain't gon' tell her, not until I know whats what. I'm suppose to be hookin' up with her Friday. We going to the beach bash at the NCO club. I know you rollin'."

"No doubt."

Allysha Hamber

CHAPTER 7

We arrived at Alicia's to pick up her and her sister Punkin. She was a full figured version of Alicia. Punkin had three golds in the front of her mouth, at least four pair of gold earrings in each ear and her hair was done up in a big blonde ponytail. She was wearing a black knitted dress that showed every curve. Some good, some that should have stayed hidden. But she was very pretty. Alicia was wearing a red fitted dress, mid-thigh length, with a six inch split on each side. She sported red pumps and her hair swept up off the back of her neck, showing her beautiful neckline. She was simply gorgeous.

From the moment they hit the car, Cory and Punkin couldn't get along. I assumed she'd had too many bad experiences with men like Cory. Every now and then she'd crack on him, calling him scooby-doo. He'd just smile and say, "Pimpin' ain't easy but somebody's gotta do it."

As we entered the club, I saw one of Terri's friends but not Terri. My heart started pounding at the thought of them meeting face to face, especially in Terri's condition. Then I thought to myself, surely Terri wouldn't be in no club pregnant. I hadn't talked to her since we went to the clinic. She hadn't called and wouldn't take mine.

I seated Alicia at the table and went to order our drinks. As I turned to go to the restroom, Terri was coming out, sponging her face. She was dressed in black spandex pants and a silk and lace top. As always, her hair was hooked but she looked a little flushed. She almost walked right past me until I grabbed her arm.

"What? You don't see me? You ain't takin' my calls, you bout to walk right by me, what's up?"

"I'm sorry, boo; I'm not feeling too good. I think I'm gonna head on home."

"What you doing here anyway? This ain't a place for you," I said pointing to her stomach. "Not no more."

"Don't start, Arman', please, I feel bad enough already."

43

I felt her head. "You do feel hot; do you need a ride home?"

I glanced over to see Alicia signaling for me to come to her. Terri noticed and placed her hand up to my face.

"Naw, you stay and have fun with yo' friends. I'm out."

"Come on, Terri. Don't be like that, baby. If you need me to go with you, I'm gone."

She lightened up a bit.

"I apologize for snapping at you. I'm just really feelin' the symptoms right now. You go ahead. I'll talk to you in the morning before you leave."

We hugged and I kissed her on the cheek.

"Drive safely, k?"

"K."

"You sure you don't need me to come?"

"I'm fine, Lynne's here."

She signaled to her friend.

"You go have fun."

She walked away.

When I went back to the table, I knew the third degree was coming from Alicia. Right on cue she snapped, "Ex'girlfriend?"

"Naw, a good friend. She's not feeling well."

"She sorta looks like the girl you were dancing with that night at the NCO club that first night we were here."

"Naw, baby, that ain't her."

"Did you order our drinks?"

"Yeah, a virgin Daiquiri on its way."

"Let's dance then."

We danced, drank and danced some more. The DJ put on KC and JoJo's, "Tell me it's real". Alicia looked at me and said, "Arman', I want you to know I'm ready to love again. I know because I'm in love with you and I wanna show you how much I love you tonight."

Great, she was ready to go to another level and I was caught up in the shit with Terri. But what could I do? I couldn't turn her down, I ain't gon' turn her down. It had been six months and if I backed down she'd know I was hittin' skins somewhere else.

"I'm ready to go, baby, how about you," she said, as she led me off the dance floor.

I stopped her at the hallway entrance. "Hold up, baby, I gotta make sure Cory has enough money to get to yo' crib."

I walked over to Cory and told him I had to holla at him. He was hemmed up in the corner booth with a fine ass Asian honey.

"Dawg, Alicia's ready to go home and do some thangs, if you know what I mean."

"Shit, it's about time, nigga. I don't know how you made it this long. I wish a woman would even think she could make me wait that long fo' some ass. I'da been gon' ghost by now. But give me yo' keys and go handle yo' biz. I'll make sure the wicked witch of the west gets back to her dungeon."

"That's cold, man."

I handed him the keys to my Elauntra. I guess Alicia and I would be cabbing it home.

As we waited outside, it started to sprinkle. A light mist covered the sky. Party goers were running by trying to get inside before the rain hit. The more it sprinkled, the curlier her hair got and the more it turned me on. I grabbed her waist and pulled her close to me. I cupped her cheeks with my hands and kissed her gently. I brought out my tongue and outlined her mouth. The rain was coming down now but we didn't move. We just stood there, tasting each other.

When our cab arrived, I was about ready to explode. As we drove along the streets, Alicia reached under my shirt and started massaging my chest. Slowly she rubbed her hands around my waist and back. She unbuckled my jeans and started stroking my jimmy, as she nibbled on my ear lobe. Her hands felt so good.

Moments later, she began biting me on the neck and I went under her shirt to touch her breasts. She moved my hand away and placed them under her skirt. I moved her panties to the side to find a cleanly shaved cookie. Inside it was warm and juicy. I twirled a finger inside her, pulled it out and placed it in my mouth. The taste was bittersweet. I placed it back inside her along with another.

"Oh, baby," she moaned.   She began to jack my jimmy faster as I continued to finger fuck her.   I glanced up at the rearview mirror and smiled.   The driver was bout to nutt on himself. Fuck it, I decided to give him something to look at.

I lifted my finger and twirled it around in a circle.   That was his signal to drive around.   He set the mood by pumping up the Quiet Storm. I tried again to touch her breasts, and again, she stopped me. What was up with that? Was they fake or something? She lifted my T-shirt and started kissing my chest. Both the driver and I wondered was she gonna do me in the back of the cab. She took out a piece of candy from her purse and placed it in her mouth. Then she softly and slowly moved to the top of my jimmy and licked it teasingly.   The cab jerked and she let out a slight chuckle.   She moaned and I moaned. She wasn't very good at giving head but she was trying to please me. I know I was wrong but I was thinking of Terri and the way she got down on my jimmy. So the moans were from mental pleasure, not physical. It was a fight to snap out of my desire for Terri and make Alicia feel special.

I began to kiss her calf. Then moved up to her inner thigh. I tried to position her comfortably in the cab so I could taste her. As soon as she spread her leg,s I was in love. It was the prettiest cookie I'd ever seen. The fact that it was soaking wet made it glisten in the streetlights. I moved my lips closer to it. Ahhhh, the smell of Summer's Eve and sweat.

I lifted her thigh up over my shoulder and stuck my tongue out to lick inside the creases of her lips. Ummmm, it tasted good. I spread the lips apart to expose her clit, which was pierced. As I played with the clit ring with my tongue, she moaned out in pleasure. I added a finger inside her and she squirmed around. She rolled her thighs and grinded them against my hand. I got pleasure from knowing I was exciting her. My moment had come. It smelled good, it looked good....dive in!

I opened wide and tried to fit her lips, her clit and the meat into my mouth at once.

"Baby that feels sooo good. Don't stop baby, don't stop."
I continued to finger her while her cookie baked in my mouth. I think I enjoyed it as much as she did.

The cab swirled again and I knew ol' boy was about to bust. I rose up, sat on the seat and put Alicia across my lap.

"Do you wanna feel it Alicia, huh? Do you want this? Tell me..."

"All of it, baby," she said as she guided my unprotected jimmy into her walls. A little loose but still as good as gold. I inched down on the seat so I could hit all up into her guts. I grabbed the back of her ass and rolled her around on top.

"Yeah, baby, take it all."

"Give it to m,e daddy...I."

Damn, why she have to say that. My mind was now drifting to Terri. The night in the park, me hitting it from the back. The sound of the nookie popping. I didn't hear Alicia cum, I heard Terri. What the hell had I gotten myself into? I was about to nutt and I grabbed her ass really hard and told her, "Take this nutt, baby. Take it all."

"Yeah, baby...take it!"
It was the cab driver. Can you believe that shit? Never-the-less, she took it like a champ.

When we pulled up to her house, Alicia sat there, still straddling me with her head on my shoulder. We fixed our clothes and I went to pay the driver. He just smiled and said, "Don't worry, it's on me. Just make sure the next time you need a cab, homey, you call for number 158."
I laughed and closed the door.

When we entered the house Cory was there and I could hear Punkin screaming for mercy. So much for that dog ass nigga huh?

Alicia and I sat down on the multi-colored couch and she ran her fingers across my waves.

"I love you and I want you in my life for a long, long time."

"No doubt, I'm here."

I began to kiss her again. We gulped, sucked and played tonsil hockey until I tried to touch her breasts again. She pulled back; I reached out to touch them once more.

"Don't..."

"What's up with you?"

"What's up is I don't want you to touch me there. It doesn't matter why, just respect it."

I raised my voice, probably more than I intended. "Oh, so the cab driver can see yo' pussy but I can't see a titty? What kinda shit is that?"

"Arman' stop yelling in my house and chill. You see what I want you to see. Don't get it twisted, just because you got some pussy; don't mean you can talk crazy to me."

"Man, I ain't got time fo' this shit, I'm out."

"Bye."

I knocked on the bedroom door and told Cory to hurry up. A few minutes later he emerged, dripping with sweat. I didn't bother saying goodbye.

"What's wrong, man? You ain't trippin' cause I hit ol' girl is you?"

"Naw, man, Alicia trippin'. All night we been freakin'. The couch, the cab..."

"The cab?"

"Yeah, nigga we straight fucked in the cab. But everytime I try to touch her titties, man, she flip out. Is it me or is that some weird ass shit?"

"Maybe her shits deformed or somethin'. Fuck all that, how was the pussy?"

"Shit, man, I kept thinkin' about Terri. I was damn near zoned out the whole damn time. Man, I feel bad, though. I shouldn't have just left like that. I'll call her tomorrow and apologize."

"What? Nigga bump that! She'll call you, trust me. She done gave you the pussy now, nigga, she ain't going no where. A playa knows these things," he said as he ran his fingers over the waves in his hair.

"Yeah," I said. I see you up to yo' usual activity. How the hell did you get her evil ass into bed?"

"I told you man, ain't no ho I can't pull playa. Daddy's just that good. Take lessons."

We got on the highway and hit Wanna Burger before I dropped him off. As soon as I got home, I tried to call Alicia. No answer. As soon as I hung up the phone, it rang back. It was Terri. I could tell she had been crying.

"I'm sorry for calling so late," she said.

"Naw, it's good. What's wrong? Still not feeling good?"

"No, but that's not why I called. I really need to talk to you. Don't say anything until I'm done, matter of fact, just listen. I've decided to keep our baby. I'm sorry if that upsets you but I can't kill my baby. If you don't want to be apart of our lives that's fine. That's your choice but I'm gonna file for an early release and raise our child. I've never told you...but I love you Arman', and no matter what you decide, I always will and our child will know about his or her daddy. Goodnight."

She hung up and I lay there and stared at the ceiling. No music tonight, just my thoughts. I started to call back but I didn't. I couldn't...it was a lack of words, not feelings. What the hell was I gonna do?

49

CHAPTER 8

In the morning, I tried to call Alicia again before I left but I got no answer. Damn Caller ID. I couldn't stop thinking about Terri's situation and the way I left things with Alicia. In the field you're outside with nothing to do but have time to think. Could I really make this work? Could I have Alicia and be a father to my shorty? What if Terri won't just accept that? I mean, most women want all or nothing. Truth be told, I loved them both. I arrived at that point for different reasons but the results were still the same. I had to try to work it out with both of them. Find some kind of common ground. I didn't want to hurt either of them.

One day after work, I decided to write them both a letter. I sat down under a big shade tree and began Terri's first.

Terri,

I wanted so badly to call back that night and tell you how I felt, but I needed time to think some things out. I'm not upset that you've decided to keep our baby and I promise that I'll do whatever you need me to do to help you through this time. I promise I'll do better at being there for you. I care for you a lot, Terri. When I get home, I would really like to sit down and talk to you.

Love, Arman'

I sat back and thought of what to say to Alicia. Should I tell her about Terri or not? Now that Terri had decided to have the bab, it seemed like the right thing to do. But often, the right thing is the hardest.

Alicia,

I need to apologize for the way things were left between us. I was trippin'. I had some shit on my mind that had absolutely nothing to do with you. I'm in a fucked up situation right now and

I can't explain. But I do care about you, a lot. When I get back, I hope we can still continue to build a relationship. For the last few months, you're all I've thought about and I don't wanna lose you. Please give me a chance to make it right.

Love, Arman'

That evening, I mailed both letters and for what seemed like weeks, I waited for their response. Their letters arrived on the same day, and when the soldier brought them to me, me eyes lit up. Finally, a chance to get this shit together. Sad to say, it wasn't quite the response I was looking for.

My dumb ass fucked around and put Terri's letter in Alicia's envelope and vice-versa. When I realized my mistake, I almost fell out. I sat down on my cot and began to access the damage.

Terri's simply read, "I'm sorry you feel you're in a fucked up situation. I'm sorry that for the past six months I've been keeping you from the one you really been thinking about and truly care about. I hope she takes you back."

Alicia's came back ripped up along with all our pictures. I was stunned at my stupidity. I fell to my knees dropped my face in my hands and wondered how I could be so damn stupid. I could feel the tears welling up in my eyes.

I wasn't sure if it was because my ego was damaged or because I genuinely felt bad for hurting them both. Maybe it was a combination of both. I had to figure this out on my own. I couldn't tell Cory cause I'd never hear the end of it. They knew about each other now. Terri, in her condition, I know was freakin' out. Although she never regulated like she was to be the only one, I knew she was still crushed. Alicia on the other hand, was under the impression that it was just us. Damn, what else could go wrong?

Once we hit the base and cleaned our equipment, we were released to go home. I went immediately to see Terri but she wasn't there. Someone had moved into her room. She'd been gone about two weeks, around the time I received her letter. I called her job and they told me she was no longer working there. She was gone. How was I gonna know if she was doing okay? If my shorty was healthy? I had no idea where she was from or anything. It was one of those times I'd wished I'd spent more time getting in her head rather than her bed. Fuck!

I went to the PX and went over to Alicia's register and asked if I could holla at her for a minute. I could see the bitterness in her eyes. She was hurt pretty badly. At first, she was hesitant but she finally agreed. I didn't quite know what to say and I tried to think it out while I waited for her outside. I'd just have to tell her, "Look baby, you wasn't givin' up no ass and I had to get it from somewhere." Naw, that wouldn't work. She might slap the shit out of me. "Baby, I'm a man, I got needs." Naw, that wouldn't work either. It was one night and the rubber popped. Yeah, yeah that's it. That'll work. Shit like that happens all the time.

When she reached me, she stood to the side of me, with her hand on her hip, neck snapping and said, "Make it quick cause frankly ain't nothing you can say that will make me understand why you been hiding another woman and a baby on the way. But you got five minutes to try."

"It's like this Alicia, it was only one time and the rubber broke…"

" Four…"

"For real, baby, I ain't playin' games with you. I met her at the club that first night I met you there. Yes, that was her you saw me talking to the last time we were there. That first night, when I saw you and Cory exchanging numbers, I thought ya'll was hookin' up and it wasn't until I saw you in the PX that day you told me ya'll wasn't. That night, after the club, I got with her and the rubba broke. I don't even know if it's mine. She left town, so I don't know. I mean, what does that tell me? But, Alicia, I'm a man, baby. If it's mines, I gots to handle my business. But it was only once baby, I swear. I want you baby. I'm tryin' to be down with you."

It was way past five minutes so I knew she was coming around. With sincere pain, I pleaded with her.

"Boo, I'm sorry. She just wasn't that important to me. You're my everything. Don't be like that."

"Not that important? In your letter you said you cared about her. How do you care about somebody after only one night?"

"You must've misunderstood the way I intended it. The only one I care for is you. Sweetheart, please don't be mad."

"I don't know. Yo' game sounds tight, but you still kept something very important from me. How am I supposed to trust you?"

"You can trust me, baby, I made a mistake."

"I don't know Arman', I need some time to think about it."

What was up with women always needing time to think about things? Usually, that means, I'm gonna make you suffer and beg to get this again. She walked away and despite my urge to call after her, I didn't. I had just laid down some major game. She'd be back...I hoped.

CHAPTER 9

A few weeks later, Cory and I went to the club. I finally told him about what happened and he told me not to sweat Terri. "She'll probably call you when the welfare cuts off, hollerin' about child support. I can't understand how women have kids against our wishes and expect us to pay child support. Them tricks is crazy man. I ain't payin' for nothing but abortions and I'm goin' with you to make sure yo' ass get it done. My sista's use to gank nigga's right and left, talkin' about they pregnant. Ain't no way poppy's fallin' for that."

"So, how many lil Cory's would be runnin' around here had you kept yo' cash?"

"Three."

"Don't you ever wonder what they would've looked like? What kinda daddy you would've been?"

"Nope."

"Damn, man, do you have a conscience at all?"

"Sometimes. Anyway, man, you the one with all the problems nigga. Don't worry about Alicia either. She'll come around too. She just wanna see you beg. Prove to her you care. Just like that shit in them romance books. Chill, show her how you roll. Don't go sniffin' up her ass or she'll have you caught up nigga. Trust me."

"I'm already caught up man, I need them both."

Every weekend it seemed we had this conversation around the table at the back of the club. I hadn't heard from either Alicia or Terri. Then I saw Alicia at the club one night but she wasn't alone. She was dancing with some broke looking run over pimp. Nigga still had on Puma tennis and an Adidas sweat suit. At least she could've flossed with a nigga that looked better than me. I grabbed a girl and hit the dance floor. Two could play the jealousy game. Who did she think she was tryin' to floss on me? Cisco's, "Thong Song" played over the speakers. Baby was grindin' all up on me and out the corner of my eye, I could see Alicia looking.

She was getting pissed. But I knew she'd never grind up on the reject from Beat Street. It wasn't her style. But I sure as hell didn't mind the way baby girl was shakin' it for me.

When the song was over, "Anytime," filled the room. As the words, "….Do I ever cross yo' mind, anytime? Do you ever wake up reaching' out for me……," pierced my heart. Alicia and my eyes met, locked and I could see all her pain and disappointment. I had betrayed her trust. She thought I was no good, a dog just like Cory. In a way, I guess she was right… to an extent.

I allowed myself to get caught up in a situation I never should've been in. But a real man handles his, regardless of the out come.

At the end of the song was over, I stepped towards her but I decided I had to come correct or not at all.

As I lay in the bed that night, the Quiet Storm kept my mind spinning over Alicia. I pictured my life with her and then without her. I was miserable without her. I had gone to bed with a few ladies here and there, trying to ease the loneliness I felt. None could match the tenderness and the love that her voice alone brought to me. She wanted a commitment. Someone to be real with her. I was ready to give her that. I didn't wanna lose her. I had already lost Terri; I wouldn't lose her too. I knew what I had to do.

I called Cory for help setting up some things and naturally I met opposition.

"I know you lyin' right? Tell me you playin'."

"Naw, man, I'm serious, I need you to help me set it up. I gotta get her back, no matter the cost."

He sighed and said, "Aight playa, if you wanna go out like a sucka then, I got yo' back. Down…."

"Like fo' flat tizes..," we said together.

CHAPTER 10

We worked out all the details and set a date for it to all go down. Once we accomplished that, I had to get Alicia's sister Punkin to help me get Alicia to the right place at the right time. At first, she was reluctant at first but once I put it down that I was serious about her sister, she came around. Plus it helped that Cory was still hittin' it every now and then.

It was all set. The night rolled around rather quickly. It was Alicia's birthday, September 25th. I was home getting dressed when the phone rang. "Hello? Hello?" No one was on the line. It rang again and again. Finally I just left the damn thing off the hook. Lately, I had been receiving the calls about once a night.

I stood in the mirror, trimmed my baby mustache and my goatee. The waves in my hair were already bumpin' so I just relined it. I dressed in crème colored silk boxers and t-shirt. A tan colored silk shirt and a crème double-breasted suit. I played a silk crème and tan striped tie and a pair of Stacy Adams.

I sported her favorite CK1 cologne; my diamond studded earring and my Rolex watch. I glanced in the mirror one more time before leaving out the door. Damn, I'm fine!

Tonight would be all good. I jumped into the Elauntra and drove to the Courtyard Marriot in downtown Temple. I went to see if Cory had made it there yet and started on his part of the evening.

When he opened the door, the smell of roses immediately hit me in the face. I walked inside and did a double take. The dining room table was set with a white silk tablecloth. It had a dozen white roses in the centerpiece, and beside it were two long stem crystal candleholders with white candles. Two crystal wineglasses held the glow of the candlelight.

The food was there ready to be served by a beautiful waitress Cory kept trying' to hit on.

I looked to the floor where Cory had a trail of white rose petals leading from the front door to the guest bedroom. I pulled the note from the door. Open the door and follow instructions.

The trail of petals left the guest room, went to the bathroom and trailed over to the dining room. I looked at him and asked, "What, no petals to the master bedroom?"

"Naw, man, you might not get no ass tonight so, I thought I'd save that seventy dollars," he said laughing.

"Naw, but for real though, you don't want her to think that this was all just to get back in her draws, so I didn't trail it to the master suite. But open the doors playa and check it out."

I walked over and opened the doors. It was beautiful. The canopy bed was covered in white silk sheets. The bed was full of pink and red rose petals. Along the dressers and night stands were more roses. I knew this would set me back a grip but I felt she was worth it.

Scented candles were on standby waiting to be lit. Cory walked in, stood in the middle of the room, clapped his hands twice and the lights shut off. The candles lit up and the stereo bumped out Eric Benet's, "Fortunate." Then he clapped his hands again and shut it all down. I turned to him and couldn't even begin to find the words to thank him. None were needed, he knew. I grabbed his hand and hugged him.

"Go get her playa."

"No doubt," I said.

"You just make sure you and that honey don't get all excited up in here."

I went to the door and stopped to call Punkin and make sure they were on time. I walked to the front desk and checked to see if the white Cadillac limo I had arranged had arrived. The clerk told me it was waiting outside.

The driver opened the door and then drove me to the NCO Club/restaurant. As the limo pulled up, all eyes turned to me. I spotted Alicia and Punkin among the long line of patrons waiting to get in. I noticed the women, pulling out their mirrors and combs, checking make-up and up-doos.

I stepped out to the whispers, "Damn he fine! Damn, who is that fine ass brotha?" I walked over to Alicia with my best "Essence" man stroll. Punkin noticed me first and her face lit up with approval. Alicia's eyes shot buck when she noticed it was me. I turned to Punkin, kissed her on the cheek and whispered, "Thank you."

"Good luck."

I turned to Alicia and extended my hand to her. She eyed me up and down, then looked at Punkin and snapped, "What ya'll up to?" She looked around me to the limo. "And, what's all this?"

"Come with me and find out," I said, extending my hand once again. The other women continued to talk.

"If she don't go, baby, I will!"

Our eyes locked and I held her gaze until her hand finally fell into mine. I led her to the limo. Punkin yelled, "Have fun, baby girl, and happy birthday."

"Arman' what is all this," she asked as I closed the limo door and we drove off.

"I guess you'll just have to trust me won't you? As a matter of fact, I have somethin' for you." I pulled out a blindfold. She pulled back and I quickly reassured her. "It's all right, baby, trust me. I just don't want to ruin the surprise."

She gave in and I tried not to mess up her hair while putting it on. I kept her blindfolded until we reached the hotel room.

Cory was gone and the waitress was out on the balcony. I took the blindfold off, put my hands over her eyes and with only enough room to see the sign on the door; I led her to the guest room. She opened the door and disappeared with the note in hand.

The instructions inside were for her to slide off her clothes, step into the shower, which was also filled with rose petals, shower and use the accessories on the counter. They included baby oil, deodorant, and a pair of nude stockings with a diamond rose on the lower right calf, a black silk and lace pair of panties and her favorite Cool Water perfume.

Alicia was instructed to put on the black velvet fitted dress with a split up to the top of the thighs. Diamond studs where placed at the base of the straps in the front of the dress. She had all her make-up and hair accessories thanks to Punkin.

Alicia was to then come to the door, knock three times and I would let her out. All this took about an hour and when I opened the door, I almost fainted at her beauty. The dress fit perfectly and complimented each and every curve on her body.

Every inch of her beautiful hair was flowing over her shoulders and she had placed the diamond clip I'd brought in the side.

No doubt, she was a complete vision of loveliness. I made a mental note to send Punkin a dozen of roses to thank her for all her help. Well, maybe a half.

Alicia stood there smiling and I extended my hand to her. I led her to the dining room table and she gasped.

"Oh, Arman' this is beautiful. Is this all for me?"

"There's more to come birthday girl."

I stared into her eyes. It was nice to see those beautiful eyes again.

"Thank you for coming with me. I've really missed you. Thank you for giving me the opportunity to be with you on your special day."

I led her over to the table and pulled out her seat. The waitress turned on the stereo and dimmed the lights. I re-lit the candles on the table. As she served dinner, "No Pain, No Gain," played the story of the past couple months of our relationship. "…We're all entitled to make a mistake, you got to prepare for some heartache. No pain, no gain…" I smiled and thought, hell of a choice "C".

Our meal consisted of Orange Chicken, wild rice, seven-layer salad, shrimp cocktail and garlic bread. After dinner, the waitress brought out the cake. A 12 x 12 yellow sheet cake topped with white icing and red roses for the trimming. The words "Only the Beginning," was in red liquid icing. The number twenty-three was lit in the center.

"Go ahead, make a wish."

"How? It's already come true. I'm here with you."

Alicia blew out the candles, cut a slice of cake for us to share and I licked the icing from her fingers. I looked down at my hands. They had not been manicured since Terri had left.

"You okay," she asked?

I glanced into her eyes. "I'm wonderful, now that I have you here with me." I told her to go grab the jacket in the closet waiting for her. "Hurry now, we have one more stop to make."

She put on the floor length velvet shoulder shawl, laced with diamonds that came with the dress. We headed back to the limo. Our first stop was the landing where we took our first stroll together.

At the entrance of the park awaited a tour guide in a lovely white carriage trimmed in gold, driven by two beautiful white stallions. Alicia grabbed my thigh like a five-year-old asking for candy.

"No we are not finna get into that carriage, baby," she said excitedly.

"Okay, we're not."

I smirked.

"Stop playin' Arman' are we? Come on," she said, pullin me towards the door. We exited the limo and the small Chinese driver greeted us, opened the door and helped us inside.

He gave us a tour through the landing and we finally stopped at the entrance to the outside Marimax Theater where the R & B group Mystic was giving a concert.

The carriage pulled to the entrance and a stocky uniformed guard told the crowd, "Make way for the carriage." Alicia's eyes popped.

"We are not going to the front?"

"Just hold on, baby. As we approached the stage, the guards pointed the way and then opened the doors to assist us out of the carriage. We were escorted to two awaiting seats on stage.

The crowd became silent as the leader said, "I see our guests of honor have arrived."

`   Alicia looked around.

61

"Who is he talking about Arman'? I know he's not talking about us is he?"

"Come on, birthday girl…no more questions."

"But how do you know Southern Mystic? How did you pull this off?"

"Baby, yo' man got mo' pull than the elastic on a fat lady's draws!"

I laughed. It was actually Cory who was good friends with one of the background singers and got me the hook-up. See, sometimes it pays to be a dog.

Once we were seated, the stage lights dimmed and one of the twins began to walk towards us. He was dressed in baggy blue jeans with rips up the side and a white wife beater.

"This is a very special night for two very special people," he began. Softly the piano began to play and Alicia's eyes lit up.

"Alicia, I want you to know that the man sitting beside you loves you very, very much. And he wants to prove that love to you. He has asked us to sing you a very special song."

Alicia glanced at me and smiled. I could see the tears forming in her eyes. One of the group members brought her a single long stem white rose. He kneeled down in front of us and in a soultrous voice, began to sing, "…….see first of all, I know these so called playa's wouldn't tell you this…"

He paused to the screams of the crowd.

"…but I'm be real and say what's on my heart. Let's take this chance and make this love feel relevant, didn't you know I loved you from the start yeah…"

It was one of Jagged Edge's classic cuts. They didn't sound as good, but it served it's purpose.

He stood up, handed me the microphone and motioned for me to stand. The crowd silenced again in anticipation to see what was going to happen next. My lady's mouth was wide open in shock. The piano played and I stared into her eyes. I was no singer but I could hit a note or two.

"...see I've done it all and frankly girl I'm tired of this emptiness. I wanna come home to you and only you. Cause makin' love to just anyone ain't happenin', I just gotta be with you..."

The group surrounded her and sung along in a whisper, "Meet me at the altar in your white dress. We ain't getting' no younger girl we might as well do this. Alicia lets get married, Arman' wanna get married."

They repeated this melody as I kneeled in front of her. I reached in my pocket and pulled out a tiny black box. Over the speakers, as I continued to stare into her eyes, which were now filled with tears, I spoke to her from my heart.

"Alicia, we've had a run at happiness and I almost lost you, because I was afraid. Afraid of loving you with every breath I take. Inhaling and exhaling your face, your body, your thoughts, your spirit, your smell and your love. It wasn't until you were gone that I realized I couldn't survive without you in my life. I never wanna suffocate again." Now, the tears were coming down both our faces.

"Will you please do me the honor of being my wife?"

As I opened the box, she opened her mouth and took in a breath of fresh air. She could hardly speak through the tears. Finally she said, "Arman', are you sure this is what you want?"

"I've never been so sure about anything in my life sweetheart."

The soloist said to the crowd, "I think she should say yeah, how about ya'll?"

The crowd screamed out, "Yyyeeeaaahhhh." I couldn't stop staring into my baby's eyes, anticipating her response. "Yes...the answer is yes! Yes, baby, I'll marry you!"

I grabbed her and kissed her to the screams of the crowd. White petals began to fall from overhead. We cried in each other's arms. Each tear filled with so much love. The group began to sing again, "........Meet me at the altar......"

We sat through the rest of the show. Towards the end of the concert, the carriage pulled back up to the front of the stage.

We were then escorted back to the entrance to our awaiting limo. Alicia was still crying off and on.

Inside the limo, my cell rung.

"Hello?"

No answer. It rang again and again, no answer. First at home, now on my cell. What was up with this shit? I was getting pissed off. The phone rang again.

"Who the fuck is this playin' on my damn phone?"

"Damn, baby, I take it she turned you down," Punkin said.

"Had to fo' this nigga to be snappin' like that. After all that shit we hooked up she said no," Cory asked?

"My bad ya'll, somebody been playin' on my phone. Hey Punkin, or shall I say sis-in-law?"

They both started hollering.

"Aw playa...you the man...you the man sittin' next to the got damn man! I'm happy fo' you, man. Now can we discuss yo' broke ass payin' me back," he laughed.

"Shut up, Cory. Oh Arman', I'm so happy for you guys. Let me talk to my sista."

As soon as Alicia touched the phone, she screamed and I could hear Punkin screaming too. I was aglow watching her smile.

She must have asked about the engagement ring because Alicia began to describe it.

"It's a half circle diamond ring, with clusters on top. The other half of the circle is on the wedding ring, so that when he places it on my finger, both the circle and our lives will be complete. Isn't that beautiful," she asked through her tears.

Alicia handed me back the phone and Cory said, "I guess I can't use that room back at the telly now, huh?"

"You damn right you can't. We pullin' up now, playa. I'll holla at you in the morning. Better yet, make that after check out time. Later."

No sooner than I hung up, the phone rung back. No answer. Alicia looked at me suspiciously.

"Who do you think it is, Arman'?"

I know who she thought it was, the same person Cory thought it was, Terri. I wouldn't believe Terri would ever stoop to that level so I told her it was probably some chick I used to mess with.

"Now, lets not let anything or anyone ruin this night for us. Come here beautiful." I held her close to me and whispered in her ear, "It get's better."

"How could this night possibly get better?"

"Just wait and see."

We exited the limo and once inside the hotel room, I took her shawl and my jacket and laid them on the sofa. I grabbed Alicia by the hand and led her to the master bedroom. She noticed the rose petals and smiled. I clapped my hands twice and the lights shut off, the candles lit up and once again the music played. I asked her to dance and I held her in my arms as tightly as I could. "…fortunate to have you girl, I'm so glad you're in my world…"

The words said everything I felt. I took a step back and glanced into her eyes. Truly happy, I cupped her face with my hands and kissed her forehead cheeks and gently on her closed eye lids. I tasted the salt from her tears.

First, Alicia took off my tie and began to unbutton my shirt. She slid it down my arms as I reached for the straps to her dress and told her, "You look so beautiful tonight. I don't know if I want to undress you or not."

"Here, let me."

She turned her back to me to undress because she didn't want me to see her. I was growing irritated and I tried to find the right way to approach the subject, remembering how it had ended before. But I ended up blurting out, "Alicia, what is it about your breasts you don't want me to see? I mean, you just agreed to be my wife and this ain't no time to be playin' shy. Talk to me, what's up?"

She stood still for a few minutes and then turned around. Her arms crossed in front of her and tears streaming down her face.

"What is it baby? I'm a man; I can handle anything you tell me. It's the not telling me I can't take. Talk to me," I said as I approached her.

She took a step back and sat down on the bed.

"Two years ago, I moved here to see a specialist for a possible mastectomy. That's when they remove one or both of your breasts due to cancer. I had a half-dollar-sized lump in my right breast that was cancerous. They wanted to remove the entire breast back home in Austin. Here, there was a specialist that said he would be able to get the lump and save my breast. So I saved, borrowed and saved some more, until I had enough to cover the portion my insurance wouldn't. It's the real reason I came here, no man, no sweetheart. I was simply tryin' to save my womanhood. He got the lump and surrounding tissue but what he didn't tell me was that by saving my breast, it would look like this..."

She dropped her hands and removed a flesh colored pad from the top of her right breast. I stood still; couldn't move. Her right breast had a huge dent in it, as if a heavy rock was resting on it. She was sobbing uncontrollably and I had to do something.

"I'm so sorry, Arman'. I put you through all that stuff about lying to me when I lied to you from day one. I just didn't wanna scare you off. "

I sat down beside her and pulled her into my arms.

"Alicia, baby, you are beautiful to me, in every way. I'm sorry if I seemed pushy, but baby, this doesn't define who you are and it doesn't matter to me one bit. I love you for you, just the way you are. I'm only concerned with your health. Are you okay?"

I put my hand under her chin and forced her to look at me.

"I feel like such a freak."

"Don't ever let me hear you say that again. You never, ever use that word to describe yourself unless you talkin' bout in the sheets."

With that, I got her to smile.

"You're the most gorgeous woman I've ever laid eyes on."

I kissed her softly and slowly then I reached up to remove her hands from her breasts. At first, she was a little resistant but I got her to relax a little. I too was a little hesitant to touch it for the first time but I was determined to make her feel special and self-confident about her body. The touch of it didn't feel that different. It was just as soft as the other.

As I continued to kiss her on the neck, I continued to massage her breasts. Sucking her ear lobes and then moving back to her neck. She tried to cover up but I took her hands and put them over her head. My hand kept them still like handcuffs. I kissed her nipple on the damaged breast first. I wanted to show her I desired her. I swirled around the nipple with the tip of my tongue and gently nibbled on the nipple with soft bites. I heard her whisper my name.

I kissed from breast to breast and I slid my hand between her thighs. She spread eagle to receive it. I used my two middle fingers to make circle eight's until she begged me to stop. Of course, I ignored her pleas and ran my tongue down her stomach to her lips. With my tongue I continued to make small circles. I placed my lips tightly around her clit and used strong sucking motions along with my fingers to bring her to peak of orgasms.

"Baby, I wanna feel you. Please, baby, let me feel you....Arman, please," she pleaded.

Before I pushed deep inside, I crawled between her legs and began teasing her with the head of my jimmy. Smooth, timely movements that took us both to unknown levels of pleasure. I put my legs on the outside of hers and closed hers so the friction from her body made it hotter and hotter. I wanted to hit her cervix.

I placed her legs on my shoulders and leaned slightly against her. Oh yeah, there it was. Each time the tip of my jimmy hit it, she moaned in ecstasy.

"I want it doggy style, baby. I want you to fuck me from the back," she said.

She got on all fours and placed a pillow underneath her stomach to hike up her pelvis. When I slid in, it was heaven. A whole new angle, a whole new pleasure. Her suction caught a hold of me and wouldn't let go.

I pumped faster and harder.

"Grab my hair," she said. I didn't respond. "Grab my fucking hair," she demanded! I gripped the back of her hair and she thrust her ass upward and backward and let it drop, which pulled my jimmy with it. Damn, it felt good. There was a freak inside her and it was dying to come out. It was my job to get her to come and play.

As I grabbed a fistful of hair, I demanded to know, "Who's pussy is this? Huh? Who's is it?"

"Yours baby. It's all yours. Get it...get it baby...harder...harder...yes...I want it in my ass...will you put it in my ass?"

There it was...the freak had arisen!!

"You sure you want that, baby? I don't wanna hurt you."

Alicia pulled off and told me to lie down. She turned her back to me and straddled me. First, she took the tip of my jimmy and put it inside of her oven to wet it. Then she scooted her legs apart and eased down.

"Damn baby, you takin' this kinda easy aren't you?"

"Trust me, I know how to satisfy myself. Do you like the way it feels? Is it tight enough for you?"

She moved up and down slightly at first, then pumped me harder and harder. She arched her back, moved her hips and took me to another world. I gripped her cheeks so hard I probably drew blood.

She motioned faster and faster. When she felt me swell, she gripped my knees and tightened her muscles to make her walls grip my jimmy tighter. She relaxed on the way down and squeezed on the way up. I was about to scream.

"Say my name. Say it," she said as she continued.

"Say it!"

"Terri. Oh, baby, I..."

The movement stopped. It seemed that in one swift move, she was standing, hand on her hip, neck swinging and cursing me out.

"What the fuck did you just call me?"

"I…"

"What the fuck did you just call me," she asked again as she stormed towards the bathroom.

"My name is Alicia muthafucka, not Terri!"

She slammed the bathroom door.

"Alicia, don't start trippin'. I'm sorry, baby. From the bottom of my heart, I am. I won't lie to you baby, Terri's been on my mind…"

"Why? Cause you wanna hit it and quit it again? Well take your sorry ass over to her house."

The door swung open.

"And, fuck her then!"

Alicia stood in front of me, tears running down her face, wrapped in a towel. "I wouldn't marry you if you were the last nigga on this earth," she snapped.

Other than that day at the exchange, we had never discussed Terri and the baby. I knew it was going to be sooner or later that it would have to be dealt with.

"Baby, please don't be like that. I've been stressin' out over Terri cause she's carryin' my shorty and I haven't heard from her and don't know what's going on. Once she found out about you, she got ghost on me. Naturally, I'm worried about her since she carrying my child. I'd be less of a man if I weren't. Look, baby, whatever Terri and I had, it's over. It was nothing, a one-night stand. I'm tryin' to spend the rest of my life with you and only you. You're my future, but I need you to understand that I would never, ever turn my back on my shorty. I won't be the sorry ass daddy that mine was. If she ever comes back and needs anything, I'm not only obligated but also committed to help her for the health and welfare of my child. And that takes nothing, nothing from the love I have for you. Look at me…"

She turned to me, tears still flowing. My eyes watered as well. Part of my tears felt bad for hurting Alicia and truthfully, some fell because of my feelings for Terri. I had to put all that behind though, if I was to hold onto Alicia.

"I love you, baby. Nothing or no one in the world could ever change that. No one. You own every vein, every muscle, and every artery in my heart. Without those, we couldn't survive. That means you are the most important thing to my existence. When I said I couldn't breathe without you, I meant it. I'm begging you..."

I cupped her face.

"Please don't suffocate me again."

She fell into my arms and I held her as tightly as I could. She looked into my eyes and I kissed her. Through salty tears, slob and runny noses, we tongued each other down as if it were our last kiss.

She grabbed my back and her towel fell. She pulled me down to the floor and took the covers from the bed. She lay in my arms and we cuddled to the music of "Incomplete."

"...I can make believe I have everything, but I can't pretend that I don't see, that without you girl, my life is incomplete..."

CHAPTER 11

"What's up playa? Give a nigga all the details."

"I'll shoot through there as soon as I drop my baby off aight?"

"Aight, peace."

When we arrived at Alicia's house, Punkin came running outside. Her and Alicia jumped up and down, screaming like they won the lottery. Punkin grabbed and kissed me on the cheek.

"Hey brotha-in-law. I'm so happy for you. You go boy!"

"Thanks, now both of you get on in there and plan our weddin'. I gotta go holla at my best man."

I kissed Alicia again, got in the car and hit Highway 35 to Cory's barracks.

"Get on in here so I can snatch off ya playboy stripes, nigga. Yo' ass is officially off the market."

"Whaddup, pimp daddy?"

"Shit, if I had yo' hand I'd throw mines in," he said laughing.

"Bullshit nigga, you ain't never givin' up the life you lead. Yo' dick gets tired to quick."

We both laughed and slapped some dap.

"You got that shit right. I can't stand the same pussy too long. Daddy needs variety. It's the spice of life ya know. Playa's move around; can't stay in one spot too long."

"You keep on and one day nigga yo' dick gon' fall off or some woman go' show up with about five bad ass bebe kids," I said punching him in the arm. "Shit man, you got me bumped. I put my seat belt on every time I pull this jimmy out the garage. And as far as five, four, three, two or even one bad ass bebe, it ain't finna go down like that. If I say I don't want no bad ass bugga snatcher,s and she has it anyway, she stuck. That's on her."

We got quiet for a minute. Cory knew I was thinking about Terri. Wondering where she was and how both her and my shorty was doing. I know I told Alicia it was a one-time thing, but Terri meant a lot to me. She had been nothing but good to me and I had no right to treat her as I did. More than anything, I felt bad for cheapening our relationship to Alicia.

Truth was, I missed Terri. My hurt turned to anger. I told her I would be by her side. Help her in anyway I could. How could she just leave like that? She said she loved me and that she cared. Well, what about my feelings? She was just as wrong as I was.

I never led her to believe that she was my one and only but I should have respected her enough to keep it real and be up front with her.

"Dawg," Cory yelled!

"My bad playa, what was you sayin'?"

He sat down beside me and grabbed my shoulder. Every blue moon, we have these very serious conversations about our lives, our futures, our dreams and our relationships. Well, mines cause the "R" word is like kryptonite to Cory.

Cory and I grew up in the same projects in Dallas. He's one month to the day older than I am. Both of our mothers were raising us as single moms. Cory was the third oldest of four boys. I was the baby under three girls. My pop wasn't in the picture since the day I was born. My moms said it was because he questioned my paternity. When I was conceived they had been going through some things. Since he was half-white, half black and my moms was half-Indian, half black he couldn't understand why his child came out with skin color as dark as a Hershey bar. Said he took one look at me and walked away.

Turned his back on a wife, four kids and all the responsibilities that came along with it. I've never seen him except on a few pictures my Big Momma had, so it's hard for me to look at him as a man. As they say, you never miss what you never had. Although, sometimes I do think of how much I missed without him.

Cory was the brother I never had. His father left behind his mother and brothers for a twenty six-year-old. When Cory was around eleven. No doubt where Cory learned his lack of respect for women. He once told me he sees them as home wreckers, nothing but trouble, so he gets what he can and bounces.

We'd spend hours talking how different we'd be when we had shorty's of our own. It was Cory who talked me into joining the military. Sitting at the neighborhood Bing Lou Chop Suey after a bug ass night at the club.

"Playa, graduation is a little over a month away and I ain't down fo' workin' at no Mickey Dee's. I'm tryin' to get up outta these projects and see some shit. Save money and move moms up outta here too. I saw this thing in the counselor's office about the Army. At the end of the summer I'm thinkin' about joinin', whaddup?"

"Shit, I don't know, dawg; I ain't down fo' no white man all up in my face talkin' shit. Do this and do that. That's some slavery shit in modern day form. Fuck that," I said drinking my soda. I thought to myself about seeing the world. He did have a point and it did sound kind of cool.

"Nigga, what you gon' do round here? These fools ain't doing nothin' but robbin', stealin' and killin'. If I don't get away from this shit, I'll be caught up in tryin' to live the fast life. I know me, you know me. I'll either end up dead or in jail. And, I ain't tryin' to go out like that. I know you ain't either."

"Hell naw, I ain't. But damn, man, I don't know bout no service. True, it's a paycheck on the regular and it would be nice to see some shit other than crackheads and graffiti. Hell, I can finally shoot me a cracka and get away with it," I said.

We slapped five and laughed.

"Naw, seriously, though, man, as long as we can stay together, I'm down."

"You know we are…"

"Like fo' flat tizes," we said together.

We asked the recruiter for our enlistment under the conditions that we hit the same duty station. Many times I wanted to give up and quit but Cory made me stick with it. He was and still is a damn good soldier. Been promoted twice in two years.

I'm at an E-3 rank, which is Private First Class, and Cory is an E-5, which is the rank of Sergeant.

Ask him anything about a Howitzer tank, an M-16 rifle or general Army history and he can tell you. Very good at what he does. He just wanna be the Mack of the world and spread himself thin. One day I wish for him to find a woman like Alicia, or even Terri, but right now he not trying to hear me.

As Cory sat there telling me how he envied my relationship with Alicia, I was shocked.

"What you have with Alicia is special, man. She's top of the line. She'll be there to support and encourage you. You know that's important as a soldier. She's beautiful and she don't take no shit off you. The one quality I wish my moms had possessed. She let my dad dog her out. He could get away with anything. I don't want a woman like that. That's why I treat'em like I do. If I know you gon' let me get over, I'm gon' get over. I want a broad with a backbone. Like Alicia. The fact that she doesn't take that shit from you means she's strong."

As I listened to him, my mind drifted to the previous night. How delicate she had been.

Cory continued, "I personally wouldn't be able to deal with her ya know, because I have to be in control of thangs. I'm not ready for that 50/50 shit. But ya'll got somethin' special. Yeah, Terri took you to that level in the sack but what Alicia don't know you can teach her. I don't see Terri coming around again, so forget about her. Don't lose Alicia again over some bullshit." He was right. Only because I didn't know where Terri was, yet whatever feelings for her I had must cease and I had to move on. I had found my queen and couldn't let her go again. I held out my hand and he dropped his inside mine.

"Thanks, playa. You know you my best man, right?"

"Aw, nigga, no doubt. You know nobody could do it better."

We embraced briefly.

"Aight, man, enough of this mushy shit. Let's hit the mall before it closes. I wanna get a pair of them new Phem jeans that hit the stores today."

Cory was already off the couch and halfway out the door. He can't stand for anyone, including me, to see him outside his playa status. My cell phone rang.

"Hello?"

No one answered. I looked at Cory and he shook his head.

"It ain't over, playa. Get ready cause it's comin'." I drug myself off the couch and we headed out the door.

CHAPTER 12

I drove along the cluttered urban streets until I reached Tiara Park Lane. The street in which I was raised. I passed a slew of houses and front yards that held so many good memories for me. As I passed a grey brick stoned two-family flat, I waved to the older frail grey-haired woman sitting on the front porch. She had her multi colored blanket thrown across her lap. It was Ms. Gladys's our long time neighbor and my mom's best friend.

You could always count on Ms. Gladys to be mom's eyes and ears when she wasn't at home. I mean Ms. Gladys told everything! She waved and smiled as I pulled into the four-bedroom brick bungalow that finally belonged to my mother.

When I stepped out the car Ma came out on the porch. My mother is only about five foot even, with a skunk like streak of grey hair going down the middle of her head. She has strong Indian features and a skin tone of reddish brown. After her gallbladder surgery, she'd picked up a little weight but she was still ever so lovely in my eyes.

She stretched out her arms to me and I retreated to the only place on earth that could always make me feel better no matter how good I already felt.

"Hey baby," she said.

"Hey Ma. How you feelin'," I asked as I kissed her on the cheek.

"I'm fine. A lil this and that but nothin' too serious that the Lawd can't take care of. You know these doctor's today, all young and fancy, don't know about spiritual healin'. My momma 'nem didn't have all these hundred'n one pills to take all the time. They's used the thangs God placed here naturally and prayed over you and by golly you got better. Now, it seems like these doctor's pump all this dope inside ya and you get even sicker. But I'm okay son, how you? You look like somethin's on ya mind."

I sat down in the porch rail.

"I'm cool, Ma. Your plants are growin' nicely."

"That's all that TLC that got'em sproutin' like that. Did you speak to Gladys?"

"Yes ma'am, I did."

"Well come on in here and let me fix you somethin' to eat. You drivin' back tonight?"

We entered the front door and I stopped to admire the changes she'd made to the house. The living room walls had been paneled and she laid down new beige carpet. The living room furniture was new thanks to my income tax check the previous year. I had purchased her a new-checkered tan and midnight blue three-piece set.

Pictures from my childhood up reflecting the growth of my sisters and me still lined the walls. Ma still had my little league football and baseball trophies displayed along the mahogany mantel.

I joined her in the kitchen.

"Yeah, I mean, yes ma'm, I gotta get on back. I just stopped through to share some news with you."

"I dreamed of fishes last night," she said, smiling as she dipped a chicken thigh in flour and then placed it in the cast iron skillet. I thought of Terri. Wondering where she'd gone and if she was okay.

"Naw, Ma. No fishes. I got one better for you though. I'm gettin' married."

She dropped the seasoned chicken leg on the counter and turned to me.

"Married? Married to who?"

"Her name is Alicia and Ma she is wonderful." Ma came and sat down beside me. "You would love her Ma, she is great."

"I'm sure she is but married, son? Are you sure you's ready for that? You know it comes with a lot of responsibility. So much that ya own father couldn't handle it."

"Ma, I'm nothin' like him thanks to you. I'm a man, a responsible man and I'm in love. We started dating and within months I knew I was in love with her. She works at the Exchange

78

in Ft. Hood. Ma...it was like I just rolled over one day and realized she was the one."

She shook her head.

"Yeah, that tends to happen. So have you met her parents yet?"

"Not yet."

"Well, at least I wasn't the only one kept in the dark, " she chuckled.

"No, but seriously, son. Only you know ya heart. And if it's tellin' you to marry this here woman than it's up to you to follow it."

She patted my hand. "And if you love her, I know I'll love her too."

"Thanks, Ma," I said as I leaned over to kiss her. I could always count on her support. We were truly blessed that way.

"But I still dreamed of fishes," she said pointing her finger.

I wanted so badly to tell her about Terri and seek her advice but I had just convinced her that I was responsible enough to get married. What would she think if I told her I had a child on the way out there somewhere? Maybe later, but not now.

I sat and enjoyed lunch with my mother. Fried chicken, rice with gravy and biscuits. We conversed about my sisters, her friends, the wedding and all the gossip about the neighborhood. By the time I left her, I was at peace about getting married. As long as I had Ma's blessing, all was well.

Allysha Hamber

CHAPTER 13

Over the next couple months, Alicia and Punkin along with my moms planned our wedding. I rarely had any time to spend alone with my fiancée because it was always the day of the dress fitting, picking out dishes, or something else going on.

Our wedding was set for the sixteenth of March. I was totally and physically committed to Alicia, yet temptation lurked around every corner. If it wasn't a fine ass woman behind the register at some store, it was a hottie at the club or a babe at the gas station. Women you wouldn't even notice if you were single, you notice in 3-D when you're engaged. Yet, it was at my bachelor's party that it was too close for comfort.

Cory was in charge of the festivities so naturally the theme was "buck wild." It was held at the Holiday Inn on Grand Ave. He had rented three suites that all adjoined. The food consisted of wings, chips, pinkie sandwiches and spaghetti. Two bath tubs were filled to the brim with MGD's, Red Dog, Colt 45, Budweiser and Old English 40oz's. The kitchen counter was packed with Seagram's Seven, Gin, Paul Mason, Remy Martin, Alize', Cisco, and of course, Crown Royal. The orange juice was out in full force.

Two of the rooms were filled with my closest family and homeys along with a ton of beautiful women. Most dressed in skimpy outfits with long hair weaves and fake finger nails. Fine, though, with major junk in the trunk.

The music selection included Luke, 2-Live Crew, DJ Quik, 69 Boyz, Mystikal and anyone who told the hotties to shake that ass. Every now and then my boy Fred, the DJ, would throw on a slow jam but only for the fellas to get their grind on. The air smelled heavily of Chronic. Couples were hugged up in the corner, on the couches, in the bathrooms and in the bedrooms. Everywhere except the master suite. Cory wouldn't let anybody back there. The body heat and sweat made it muggy inside the room so I stepped outside onto the balcony.

Cory came out and tapped me on the shoulder.

"I know you ain't out here by yo'self when I spent all this money to throw you a party?"

"It's hot in there, man. I needed some air."

"Yeah, I hear you. Some of them nigga's left the crib without protection, if you know what I mean," he said pointing at his arm pit.

I glanced at the buildings lit up in downtown Dallas. It was beautiful. I thought of Terri. Cory handed me a glass of Alize' as I turned to him and asked, "Do you think I'm doing the right thing? I mean man; I don't think I'm ready for all this yet. Be all up under one woman 24-7. What if I get bored? You said yo'self yo' dick gets bored after hittin' the same shit all the time. What if she gets bored and fucks around? I mean…"

"Chill nigga, you stressin' over silly shit. Yeah, my dick gets bored but you ain't me. You've always been able to handle relationships, I haven't. You know this is the right thing to do. You about to spend the rest of yo' life with a woman so flossy, not one of us in this telly could pull. Every doubt you havin' needs to cease cause it don't get no better, dawg."

"Yeah, you right, playa. Thanks, man."

"Yeah, yeah, no gay shit. Drink up. Tonight's yo' last night of freedom and guess what daddy's got in store for you?"

He pointed inside the room and my cousin Derrick opened the back bedroom door. Out came a woman, around 5'8, 180 pounds of the hottest, sexiest, desirable, down right baddest chick you ever laid eyes on. Light brown skin like caramel. Hair hangin' mid back level. Face made up beautifully with perfect colors. She wore a black leather teddy with a slit down the front, exposing her lovely round breasts, with a black leather garter on her thigh. Her smooth set of legs accented by a pair of leather open toe pumps. She carried a leather whip in her right hand.

Cory pushed me inside and directed me to the couch and told Fred to pump up the music. He put in "How Do You Want It." She lifted her leg and placed her foot on the couch beside me. As Pac spit out the bombest rap, "…I love the way you activate yo' hips and put yo' ass out; got a nigga wantin' it so bad I'm bout to pass out..."

She moved in an up and down motion using the whip as her toy. She turned around, bent over and hiked her ass in my face. She began to shake it so fast; I swear I felt the couch vibrate. I could see the size of her cat swelling on the side of her thong.

When Cory moved the table behind her, she stepped back and placed the whip between her legs, rocking back and forth. "...I love the way you flaunt it..."

She must have read my mind as she came to me. She leaned in, gripped the whip and slid it under my nose. Side to side she tugged as she whispered.

"Smell good, huh?"

I closed my eyes and absorbed the intoxicating smell of her body. I moaned in agreement with her. The fellas were screaming, "Let me smell, let me smell."

Nigga's was flashing fifties and hundred dollar bills in the air. She made her way back to the middle of the floor and began a seductive dance to "Twelve Play."

"......Twelve, that's when I'll go down on my knees, giving you some of my twelve play..."

She was straddling me facing forward, spread eagle and grinding all over me. She took my drink and handed it to one of the boyz behind me. She rose up, turned towards me, took my hands and placed them on her breasts.

The fellas cheered for me to take off the teddy she was wearing. I slid the straps off her shoulders releasing a set of the prettiest breasts I'd even seen.

For a brief moment, I thought about Alicia. Only for a moment as Passion, the tattoo on her right breast labeled her, began to shake her silicone filled melons in my face. The faster she shook, the louder the cheers came from the fellas.

Cory walked up behind her and poured champagne down her breasts causing it to flow all over my face. I opened my mouth to taste it and swirled my tongue up and down her cleavage and across her nipples. I bit down on them gently.

She pulled off my t-shirt, rubbed her hands across my chest and made sure I felt every inch of her nails. I gripped her ass as she took her tongue and touched the tip of her nose. Daaammmmmnnnn!! I bet she was dangerous with that thing.

She unbuckled my jeans and held up her hand. Cory gave her a can of whip cream and she sprayed it around the slit of my boxers. She pulled out my jimmy and began to smile. She started at my face, moved down my neck and didn't stop until she reached the lining of my boxers. My boyz had my arms pinned down so I couldn't move. First, she licked all the cream off, before placing two cubes of ice in her mouth.

I trembled from the coldness of the ice mixed with the heat of her jaws. It immediately made my toes curl. My boys was clappin' in the background and Cory was giving her instructions.

"Make it feel good to him baby. He's off the market tomorrow, so make him memba this night."

She took it all the way to the back of her throat and my mind flashed to Terri. I sat there wondering if she was loving on some man like she once loved on me.

She began to hum, causing my jimmy to vibrate inside of her mouth. I clinched my fist and tried not to explode in everybody's presence. Cory shouted, "Okay, baby, enough of that. Time to take him to heaven." He dropped a roll of condoms six deep. Do yo' thang, boy."

She pulled me off the couch and led me to the master suite. As usual, Cory had it hooked. Champagne on ice, massage oil, the whole nine.

She took me over to the bed and sat me down. She picked up a strawberry and placed it inside her mommy to wet it and then placed it in her mouth. My mouth was watering just imagining the flavor on that berry. UMMM!!

As she danced to R Kelly's, "Honey Love," she grabbed the oil and began to oil her body down. She stepped over to the bathroom door and turned to me.

"You seem like a handful," she said looking at my jimmy. "I'll need more help."

She opened the bathroom door and exiting was a half Puerto-Rican/half black sister along with a light skinned sister. Two beautiful creatures. The mixed sister was wearing a leather bikini set. On the lower part of her back was a flossy tattoo of a hundred dollar bill. She was gulping down champagne.

Her partner had on nothing but glitter around her nipples and around the triangle shaped hair on her mommy. She was on the thicker side. Booty and thighs like what? I mean ass for days!

Her hair was cut in a crop style hook up dyed blonde. She had a tattoo on her right thigh that read, "Pretty's Breezy." In the hood, Breezy translated as bitch. Who ever Pretty was, she belonged to him or her. Fine by me, cause that night she belonged to me.

As the light skinned sister took off my shoes, my pants and my boxers, my heart sped up and palms got sweaty. She pulled me from the bed, while the half breed sister brought a chair over and placed it directly in front of the bed. She kissed me on the chin and handed me a glass of champagne.

"Sit back and enjoy the show."

When Breezy climbed in the bed, Passion was lying across the top. Passion motioned with her index finger for Breezy to come closer. Breezy crawled to her as she opened her legs.

They began to kiss. Tongue touching, swelling and dancing with each other. They caressed as I watched intensely. Shit like this only happens on my freak flicks at the crib. Now, here it was happening before my very eyes.

Half Breed was behind me, massaging my shoulders. She walked around me, dipped a strawberry in the champagne and fed it to me. She retrieved the massage oil, stood in front of me and stared into my eyes as she poured the oil down her chest. Slowly she massaged the oil over her breasts and arms, making her body glisten in the candle light. She moved to the sounds of After 7.

She turned her back to me, poured the oil down her legs, bent down and rubbed it into her beautiful skin. Beginning at her ankles she traveled to the top of her thighs, spreading her lips apart and sliding her middle finger inside.

Over the horizon of her ass I could see Breezy kissing Passion's breasts. Passion stroked her head as Breezy slid her fingers between her thighs.

Half Breed walked over to the bed and rubbed oil on Passion's breasts as Breezy nibbled with kinky passion. This shit is off the chain, I thought. I ran my hand down my jimmy and slowly began stroking it. I watched Half Breed massage oil over Breezy's back side. She moved down her thighs and spread Breezy's pink, cleanly shaven cookie. Half Breed massaged Breezy's mommy while Breezy rotated her head between Passion's thighs.

I got up out the chair and walked over to the bed. I craved a closer look. Breezy had Passion's lips spread apart and was beating her clit with her tongue. She had two fingers inside her and Passion responded with the movement of a gypsy.

Half Breed was fingering Breezy from the back. I walked around to the back of the bed, still stroking my jimmy. Breezy possessed a beautiful sparkle from the oil.

My jimmy was swelling near eruption as I saw one finger in her mommy and one in her ass. Visual stimulation is a muthafucka! They were straight working each other.

Half Breed sat down on the bed, surrounded my jimmy with her hand and pulled it to her. She swirled her tongue around the head, then slid my jimmy into her mouth. She knew how to work her muscles in her jaws allowing my jimmy to just float in and out her mouth.

I watched their faces and their bodies moving Passion near her peak, Breezy rotating her thighs and her neck. Half Breed, jaws moving in rhythm, in and out, out and in. It made the feeling more intense. My body heated immensely, and once again, I felt the pressure and sensation build. Before I could release Passion moaned, "Don't be stingy girlfriend. I wanna taste him too."

She released me and guided me to the front into Passion's awaiting mouth. She then walked over to the dresser and pulled out a chocolate colored strap-on. About seven inches in length, she stepped inside and snapped it's buckle. It looked almost as real as mine. My heart was beating from the pleasure of Passion's mouth, mouth watering from watching Breezy lick Passion's clit and imagination running wild watching Half Breed enter Breezy from the back. Breezy raised her head, looked around to Half Breed and said, "Yeah, gimme what you got."

"Oh, I plan to. I know what you like."

The way she stroked Breezy from behind was so natural. She had a style so smooth. When she stroked soft and slow, Breezy returned to pleasing Passion, who in turn, was doing her best to suck my insides out. When Half Breed put it down, Breezy's vocals rose to let out her moans of doggy style gratification.

It was like a chain reaction…first Passions screams were felt in the tightness of her jaws around my jimmy. The suction became too hard to fight. I let it loose. A nutt so big, it took her two gulps to get it down. It seemed to last forever as I watched Half Breed bring Breezy to her peak.

I took a step back. I needed to sit down, my head was light. Breezy grabbed me, "Wait, poppy, where are you going? The funs just getting started. I haven't gotten my chance to feel you."

I stared at the condoms on the night stand. Half Breed handed me another glass of champagne and kissed me on the cheek.

"Come on, tiger, let's play."

Passion and Breezy pulled me down on the bed and began to kiss all over me. Two different women, two different tongues, same pleasure. It was at that moment I realized that no matter how many women I lay down with, they all possess the same thing. They may move and use it differently but it's all the same. Mentality plays the major role. It's how you feel about that person and perceive her that truly brings the pleasure. How beautiful she is, how sweet she sounds when she whispers your name, how sexy her body is, and basically feeling good simply because you're making the one you love feel good. I shared that with not one of these women. I shared it with two and one of them was gone, so it was only Alicia I desired.

"Ladies, I appreciate the excitement and I thank you for making this a night I'll always remember. But, I'm going in the other room and rest up for my big day tomorrow," I said pushing them to the side.

"But, poppy, we just wanna have a little more fun with you. Can't you stay a little longer," Breezy asked.

"Naw, ladies, I can't but hey, there's plenty of guys out there who'd love to take my place."

I slid on my shorts and opened the door. No sooner than I shut it behind me, Cory approached me.

"Hoooo, big daddy! You look like you just handled yo' business real propa like. You the man...hell yeah you the muthafuckin' man!"

He slapped me on the back. He was high as hell with a six inch blunt hanging from his mouth.

"Naw dawg, I passed. But they lookin' for a partner to finish what I started. Be my guest."

"What the hell is wrong with you nigga? Them three of the baddest bitches in Texas. You buggin' man, how can you turn down a trio of pa-dussy?"

He shook his head as he inhaled his herbs. "Damn, nigga, you done gone soft on me. Take yo' cotton ass on in there and go to bed." He pushed me into the room and closed the door. I plopped down on the bed as he yelled, "Aey, niggas, free pussy in the back!"

Then I heard a stampede of drunk ass perverts bum rushing the room.

I lay there, proud of myself in a way; mad at myself in another. I had every man's fantasy. Three fine ass women who definitely gave me a show to remember but it was my baby who had my heart. Thoughts of her ran through my mind as I drifted off to sleep; which didn't take long, thanks to champagne, Passion, Breezy, Half Breed and the soulful sounds of the Pied Piper.

"...all you have to do is just call me, I'll be there for you, it's true, only for you..."

I felt the warmth of her arms, I saw the beauty of her face, and I heard the softness of her voice…only it wasn't her…it was Terri.

Allysha Hamber

CHAPTER **14**

Nine a.m., my wedding day, Cory woke me up with one of his concoctions to rid me of the hang over I had. My head felt like I had been through a gang initiation. It was pounding but my memory was in tact. I closed my eyes again and thought back to last night. Breezy, Passion and Half Breed…ump, ump, ump!
Cory slapped me and said, "Come on, man, you don't wanna be late fo' your weddin'."

It was set for one o'clock. I pushed back the covers and sat up. He handed me the glass and gulped it down. I don't know all the ingredients, but I do know Tabasco sauce was one of them. Whatever it was, it mixed with the taste of my morning breath was about to make me throw up. I got my shaving kit and headed for the shower. I lined up my goatee, brushed my teeth and stepped in the shower trying to wash away the past.

From last night, to the first night I became a man, it all had to go. I was now a committed man. As the water ran down my face, I thought back to each and every chick I'd ever been with. There wasn't a whole lot but there was enough.

I lost my virginity to my seventeen-year-old cousin who my momma left home to baby sit us when she hit the corner tavern every first of the month. Her name was Ta'tionna. She was a senior in high school and had all the neighborhood boys after her. Cory and I thought she was the prettiest thing walking. I was in the seventh grade at the time.

The night she took my virginity, she came into the bathroom, reached down inside the water and pulled on my jimmy. I jumped up and put my hands over my private parts and said, "What's wrong with choo girl?"

"Shh, Porsche 'em sleep. Chill Manni, Don't be scared."
She ran her finger down my fragile chest. "When I finish with you, you gon' be the biggest playa this side of D-town."

She grabbed my hand and pulled me out of the tub. Water dripping, heart racing, body freezing, pee wee hanging, (or shall I say angling). She led me to a pallet of blankets on the front room floor.

"Lay down," she said.

I got down on the floor and covered myself with the top blanket. I was scared and I was shaking. Partly because I was cold and partly because I was nervous. Te-Te, as we called her, stood above me and unzipped my momma's bathrobe. She was naked. My eyes lit up cause she looked like the girls in Cory's magazines. She had real breasts and hair around her pocket book as my moms called it back then.

I kept thinking, wait 'til I tell Cory, he's gonna flip. She kneeled down beside me.

"First let's move all this cover," she said. She stared at me for a minute and once again she grabbed my junior. It felt funny but in a good way. Within seconds, it was solid, just like some mornings when I woke up.

"You have a nice sized thing Manni. I bet it feels good too. Come'mere, let me make you a man."

She laid down and pulled me on top of her. She spread her legs and reached down to guide my junior inside her. It was slippery and hot.

It made my body heat rise and with her hands placed on each side of my waist, she taught me the rhythm she liked. Up and down, fast and slow. She began to make noises like the women on TV. I thought I was really handling my business then. I stroked harder as the heat inside me continued to rise.

I felt a pressure in my stomach as well as sickness. My head became light and I was getting weak but it felt good. Then I felt like I had to pea really bad. The pressure felt like my bladder was about to burst. The more I humped, the more the sensation rose and the harder I had to concentrate on keeping it in. I didn't want to squirt it out on her.

As she moaned louder and louder, her insides got hotter and hotter. I couldn't hold it any longer. BOOM!! I got up and ran with shit spurting everywhere. I thought I was peeing all over myself. I stood over the toilet and waited for the rest to come out but nothing came except milky white, slimy gook.

Te-Te was calling after me. "Manni, it's okay. Come'mere let me tell you what happened."

I couldn't move. As the cream flowed from my junior, I felt paralyzed. It felt like it was literally draining me. I was breathing heavy and I couldn't slow down my heartbeat. I felt like someone was pulling everything from within me. Te-Te came into the bathroom and put her hand on my shoulder.

"It's okay Manni, you just came."

I looked at her confusingly. "Where I go?"

She laughed.

"This," she said as she put the hanging sperm on her fingertip.

"Is sperm. It's okay, it's supposed to come out. It's how you as a man are able to make babies."

"I know that, I just didn't know how it was suppose to feel when it came out. I thought I had to pea."

"You'll get the hang of it," she said as she walked out.

"Stop standing there looking stupid. Get to bed before Auntie gets home."

I couldn't sleep, I felt funny. I lay there and smiled. I was a man, my junior was now my jimmy and I'd had sex with a girl that all the nigga's wanted. I had to tell Cory; I couldn't wait to see him in the morning.

"Get the fuck outta here," he said as I told him the details of the previous night.

"For real, man, I swear. I was tearin' it up! Had her hollerin'."

"Whatever, nigga, if you humped her for real then, was it dry or was it wet?"

"Wet...and sticky."

"What did you feel on your thing when you got inside her?"

"Fire. Oh, and it kept hittin' this lil bump in there. I don't know what it was, but every time it touched it, she hollered more."

He laughed.

"Aaaawww shit, my man! You did hit it! Welcome to the playa's club."

Shit, I was the man after that. I had a main girl all the way through high school named Vanessa but Te-Te and me still hit it every month until she left for college. I had begun to experience a lot of things but the one thing I didn't experience with anyone even Vanessa was love. Yeah, I cared about her and a lot of other chicks but so far in my life I knew love, real love with only one woman. It took twenty-four years and Alicia for that to happen. I was ready to do this. Ready to grab hold of the love I had for her and keep her near me forever.

CHAPTER 15

When we arrived at Sunrise Baptist Church, known to us as "the little church on the hill," most of the guests were already there. I looked through the crowd and located my mom and Ms. Jackson, Cory's mom. They both had on beautiful white dresses, laced with pearls, huge purses and hats big enough to be beach umbrellas.

"There's my baby. Look at you, all grown up and getting' married. Oh, baby, momma's so proud of you and you's doing the right thing. That Alicia is a lovely girl and she'll make you a good wife. Maybe, I'll get me some grand babies now..."

As she talked, I thought of Terri. I knew she had to have had the baby by now. What was it? Where were they? How was she? How could I just move on with my life knowing they were out there, maybe in need of me? What would my momma think of me if she knew about them, the grandchild she already has? Ohh, the drama!

"I'm so proud of you, son. Now, if we can just settle this one down and find him a good woman," she said pinching Cory's cheeks.

"Aw come on now Ms. Jones. You know I ain't no one woman man," he said kissing her on the cheek.

"Ozell girl, give it up," Cory's mom said.

"I done told this here baby of mines too many times. If he keeps messin' round with these young gals hearts and thangs, somebody's gon' make me childless. They calls my house all times of the night. Won't give 'em his number. He don't wanna be bothered, Cory would rather they bother me."

She looked at Cory and grabbed him by the chin.

"It's a thin line between love and hate, boy."

"Don't start with me, momma. Besides, you know you my one and only anyway."

Cory kissed her.

"Come on, man, we gotta bounce and get you ready. Hold up man. Damn…," Cory said slapping his hand into my chest.

"What?"

"There go, Pooh. Damn she fine as hell! Never could get at that. She never would give in, talkin' bout I'm like her brotha and shit. Damn that! Man, just look at her…ump!"

I laughed at Cory's animation as he talked.

"You mean to tell me there's two in this world you couldn't pull? Playa, whaddup? You loosing yo' touch boy," I told him.
Up walked my second oldest sister Pooh. She stands 5'4, around 140 pounds, pretty brown skin with long dark eyelashes like my moms. Her hair cut in layers and wrapped. Pooh is a body-piercing turnout. She has a clip in her right eyebrow, about four holes in each ear, a bar-bell in her lower lip, a nipple ring and her latest I heard was somewhere I'd rather not know. Pooh was carrying her bride's maid dress in her arms.

"Hey lil brotha," she said as she hugged me.

"You nervous."

"Nah, I'm cool." I looked over her shoulder. "Where's Kev?"

"On the curb where I kicked his sorry ass, " Pooh laughed.

"Umm," Cory interrupted.

"Well sexy chocolate if you're in need of an escort for the day or…say the rest of your life by all means, please allow me to volunteer for the job," Cory said as he kissed her hand. He pecked his lips up her arm as she smiled and I laughed.

"How many times I gotta tell you girl, you'll never be happy cause I'm the one you need to be with. I'm the one, the only one who can make you happy."

Maybe I was trippin' cause for a minute, I thought he was dead serious.

Pooh dropped her smile, looked from him to me. I shrugged my shoulders.

"Don't tell me you're slowin' down?"

She looked him up and down.

"You are lookin' rather handsome these days. Manni, give him my number. That way if it goes bust I can blame you," Pooh said, polking me in my chest.

She looked at Cory and slid her finger down his cheek.

"Call me."

"No doubt baby." He looked at me, smiled and winked his eye. "Told you boy...not one."

After we mingled a little more, Cory and I headed for the dressing room. My phone rang along the way.

"Hello?"

No answer. It rang again and music played in my ear. "... Congratulations, I thought it should've been me, standing here with you. Congratulations..."

I stood paralyzed for a moment. Could it really be Terri? Naw, it couldn't be. How would she know I was getting married? I sat the phone down on the table and walked over to my tux hanging on the rack across the room. As I unzipped the suit bag I asked Cory to see if Alicia was there. He returned a few moments later.

"Yeah, her and the posse is down the hall."

I flew past him down the hall and knocked on the door.

"Alicia it's m,e baby, I'm cumin' in."

"Ohh, no you ain't! It's bad luck to see the bride before the wedding."

I knew that voice. It was Te-Te. Who would have thought that she would be apart of the wedding.

"Okay then, come to the door."

Seconds later I heard the voice of an angel.

"Hey, how's my husband to be?"

"Propa, now that I've heard your voice. I've missed you all night."

"I've missed you too," Alicia said.

"I can't wait to see you."

"Me neither."

"I love you," I told her.

"I love you more."

I placed two fingers to my lips, kissed them and put them to the door. I was ready. I walked to the room to get dressed.

My tuxedo was black with a mid length tail. A hunter green tie and cumber-bun accented the white shirt underneath. I sported black Stacey Adams for my big day, along with my diamond tie clip and Rolex watch. Cory's tux was the exact duplicate of mine.

Once we got dressed, we were on our way out the door and my phone rang. No one there. It rang twice more. "Hello?"

Again, no answer. Deep inside I think I prayed it was Terri. Just let me hear your voice; let me know you're okay. "Don't start trippin' playa, let's go. Hold up a minute...let me look at you."

He glanced up and down, frowned and shook his head.

"What," I asked.

"What the hell wrong with you? Why you lookin' at me like that? I gotta a booga in my nose or somethin'?"

"Naw, it ain't that...somethin's missin'," he said with a sly smirk on his face.

"What," I said checking myself over.

He reached in his pocket and pulled out a tiny black box. He handed it to me.

"What, nigg? You proposing to me?"

We laughed.

"Just open it, nigga."

I opened the box to find a one-carat diamond earring, made in the shape of a tire with gold spokes. "Aw dawg, dawg, this is tight. Man this is flossy. What the hell made you..."

I looked up at Cory and he smiled. Then he turned his head to the side for me to see the mate. I smiled and he looked at me.

"We been boyz since we were yea high. I can't go back in my mind and think of one time when you didn't have my back. You my homie, my ace-boon-coon, my brotha and my nigga for life. And I'm so happy for you, man. As long as I have this one," he said pointing to his ear.

"And you have that one, we'll always be connected. Down..."

"Like fo' flat tizes," we said.

He grabbed my hand and we hugged. Simultaneously we sniffed.

"You cryin' playa," I asked.

"Hell naw, nigga, I got sinuses."

"Since when?"

I laughed and he punched me in the arm.

"Come on playa let's do this."

As we walked out the door, the phone rang again.

"Don't even answer it, dawg. Let's go."

I walked towards the table to pick up the phone.

"And leave that muthafucka here!!"

CHAPTER 16

The chapel was decorated in hunter green and white. Ribbons and flowers decorated each row. A white roll of paper was laid down the center aisle. Hunter green and white balloons were all along the walls, accented by beautiful floral arrangements including my baby's favorite whit roses.

The rented piano was white with hunter green flowers thrown across the top and ribbons on the side. The altar was decorated with roses sprayed hunter green with a base color of white. It was all simply beautiful.

Reverend Carter, who had been my Pastor since childhood, greeted me at the door and showed me to my place. I scanned the guests and posed briefly for pictures.

I was cool until the first piano key was struck. My stomach tied up in knots and my heart raced rapidly but I stayed composed. After all, I was there, I was willing and I was ready.

My cousins Polky and Mann walked my mom and Alicia's mom to their seats. Both wee already shedding tears. I blew my mom a kiss. The music played as Pun and Cory, best man and maid-of-honor strolled down the aisle. They made a flossy couple. Punkin had stars in her eyes like she was getting ideas while Cory was busy posing for the cameras and winking at all the women in the passing rows.

Next, my two sisters came down the aisle escorted by a couple of my homeboys and Alicia's cousin. Afterwards, her niece Desire' came spreading her white and green petals along the way, followed by my nephew Dorian the ring bearer.

Once he was in place, Rev. Carter asked the church to stand. My cousin Tony walked over to the piano and began to serenade us while the baby grand played the melody to "Here and Now."

"...One look in your eyes and there I see, all that a love should really be..."

The door flew open and in came my angel. In her floor length silk white laced gown, with an eleven foot train was my bride. Alicia's hair was done up on pin curls with white baby breaths. Her veil wasn't the traditional over-the-face deal. It had a lace band with crystal rhinestones and the veil itself hung from the back of her head underneath her waist. Escorted by her father Philip in an all white tux, Alicia looked exquisite. Her face had a glow of pure beauty, and when they reached me, the serenade ended. Rev. Carter asked, "Who gives this woman to this man to be wed?"

"I do," her father Philip answered. He placed her hand in mine as he looked to me.

"God bless you son."

He kissed Alicia and walked over to the bench to join her mother. We turned to face the Pastor but not before I took a moment to admire the wonderful vision in front of me. One I'd wake up to every morning for the rest of my life.

"Let us bow our heads in prayer," Rev. Carter said. I gripped Alicia's hand and closed my eyes, to thank God for this day, this gift.

"Heavenly Father, we come before you as humble and meek servants to Your will. Lord we ask you to bless this union between Your son and Your daughter on this day. To watch over this service and Thy will be done. Amen."

He raised his arms.

"Dearly beloved, we are gathered here today to join in Holy Matrimony, this man and this woman. If anyone can state their claim as to why this couple should not be joined together, speak now or forever hold your peace."

"Oh my God...oh God...somebody help me!" A voice shouted. "Is there a doctor in the house? This lady needs help! She's about to have a baby."

My neck snapped, my heart raced and I couldn't move. I couldn't see through the crowd that gathered to see who it was but I had a feeling. And it wasn't a good one. Cory pushed through the crowd as I stood paralyzed in fear. Cory rushed back to me and said, "Oh, shit! Excuse me Lord. Dawg, you'll never guess who that is…"

"Don't say it," I pleaded.

"Yep, and she's about to blow. You betta go handle it. I'll stay here with Alicia."

There was so much noise, people yelling and screaming. "Who is she," everyone asked. I looked to Alicia, her eyes beginning to water. I stepped towards her and reached for her.

"Alicia, I'm so sorry, I didn't…" Cory stepped between us.

"Go on, man. I'll handle this. It'll be aight. Trust, handle that and get back up here nigga, pronto!"

As I pushed through the crowd, I heard someone say they called the ambulance and it was on its way. When I reached Terri I almost passed out. It is her. Her face was hunched up in pain, dress soaked and yet she still managed somehow to be beautiful.

"Arman', help me," she cried. When she shouted out my name, my momma and my sisters all looked at me. "Please Arman', help me."

"Manni, who is that," Pooh asked. I couldn't answer.

"What's going on son," Momma asked me gently through all the noise and commotion.

"She's an old friend, Ma. And from the looks of it," I paused. "You're about to be a grandmother."

"What?"

They all yelled in unison. The came the questions, a hundred and one of 'em. All the while, Terri was crying out in pain.

"I'm sorry, Arman'. I'm so sorry."

"Momma please, I need to handle this. Please, can you move all these people back? I promise I'll explain this to you when this all calms down."

She looked at me through disappointing eyes.

"I promise, Ma."

She shook her head and began to break up the crowd. As Alicia's parents walked by, I could hear her mother calling me every trifling nigga in the book. They walked over to console their daughter. I stood their overwhelmed by the fact that Terri was there in front of me and about to deliver my shorty. I kneeled down beside her.

"Terri, what are you doing here? How did you get here? Why did you leave like that? Why didn't you call, leave an address or somethin'?"

"OOHH," she screamed.

"Okay, okay I'm sorry. We can talk about that later. Are you okay?"

"No. I'm having a baby and it hurts! Please get me some help."

"The ambulance is on its way bay, you just hold on. I'm right here, I ain't going any where. Just hold my hand." She squeezed my hand and almost crushed my fingers. "Okay, hold my wrist. Let go of the hand, wrist Terri, wrist."

Terri had sweat running from her forehead and I took my handkerchief from my tux pocket and wipe her brow. I sent the church nurse for a blanket and a cup of ice because she complained of her throat being dry. I didn't really know what was happening or what to do. In between her pains, I tried to talk to her.

"I know this is the wrong time Arman' and I'm really sorry. I thought I'd make it through the wedding ceremony before the pains got too bad."

"You mean you were in labor when you got here?"

"Since about nine this morning. But I wanted to be here on your special day."

"Terri..."

"Its okay, Arman', it took a couple of months to get over it but I made it. I...ooohhh...oooohhh...another one's coming...ooohhh!"

"Terri, I need you to understand, I..."

"OOOHHH..."

I looked up to see the nurse coming through the door with the blankets in hand followed by Alicia. Her make up was smeared in tear stains down her face. Alicia was standing there in her gown, twirling her engagement ring around her finger. Her eyes sprung forth fresh tears as she looked at me, then to Terri, and back to me.

I put my leg up to stand and she quickly put both of her hands up to stop me before she turned to leave.

"Alicia, don't go…wait."

She left, passing the EMT's on their way inside.

"Okay Terri, the ambulance is here. I'll be out in a sec."

"Arman', no! Go get your wife, I'll be fine. Don't worry about me. Go…"

"No, you're not gonna have my baby without me. I'll fix this with Alicia later. Just let me holla at Cory first and I'll be right there."

They loaded her on a stretcher and I headed to the back room to find Cory. He was sitting out on one of the chairs talking to Pooh.

"C, man let me holla at you for a minute."

Pooh stared at me with a disgusted look.

"Whaddup, playa? I tried to holla at Alicia man but she ain't tryin' to hear nothin' on yo' behalf."

"Straight?"

I sighed.

"Well, that's cool. I'm about to roll up to the hospital with Terri right now. I'll fix this other shit later. Just hold down the fort 'til I get back. And try to explain this to her if you can," I said looking to Pooh.

"Man, I don't know what to say. It's fucked up she pulled this shit. She knew what she was doing. Hoes is smart."

"Man, what I tell you about…"

"My bad, but damn, broads will fuck up a wet dream. Trust me, she knew this was gonna come tumblin' down. Watch yo'self, playa, that's all I'm sayin', watch yo'self."

We hugged.

"When you get there, hit me on the hip and I'll bring the family, aight?" Cory said as I walked away.

"Cool."

I ran out the door and jumped in the Elauntra to follow the ambulance. I sped behind them, lights flashing, running all kinds of signals and stop signs, thinking about what was about to happen. I was also thinking about Alicia. I mean this wasn't my fault and what exactly did she expect me to do? Was I supposed to turn my back on the woman who was about to give birth to my child? What kind of man would she be marrying? She had to understand.

When we pulled into the emergency room parking lot, I parked near the door, jumped out and caught up with them at the entrance. Terri was in constant pain. The medic told the ER doctor she was eight centimeters dilated and near crowning. That meant they could see the baby's head and delivery was near.

When we got on the L & D ward, she was rushed inside a room for an examination and I was directed to a scrubbing sink and was told to gown up.

"Gown up? For what?"

"You the father?"

"Yeah but…"

"Gown up then soldier, she's gonna need your support."

I put on the powder blue gown, mask and shoe covers the husky white male gave me. I scrubbed my hands, arms and nails.

"Let's go, we don't have much time," the nurse said.

The delivery room was a private suite decorated with Mickey Mouse and Minnie Mouse. It was very warm inside. They had Terri laid up in the bed with her legs in stirrups and a sheet covering her. There was an IV in her arm and a nurse at her side placing a small monitor on her stomach. Thump, thump, thump, thump, thump. It sounded like a set of drums. I stood still. It was the sound of my shorty's heartbeat. Beating at least a hundred times a minute.

Terri looked at me, and for the first time since all this madness began, we smiled. They had given her something for the pain and she was a lot calmer now. She held out her hand to me and I went to her side.

"Okay, Ms. Lambert, we're ready to begin pushing on the next contraction. Dad, when she begins to push, I want you to grab the leg closest to you and pull it to her chest, slowly. Ready?"

"Uh-huh," she said. I didn't know what to expect. A part of me felt I shouldn't be there. But that thought quickly vanished as she began the first push. She inhaled a deep breath, let out a big push and as the sweat came running down her forehead.

"Good...good," said the doctor.

"Hold it a little longer...good, good. Okay, you can relax."

"You okay," I asked, as I wiped her head and massaged her thigh.

"I'm fine. Thank you so much for being here. I didn't want to go through this by myself...oh doctor, I'm feeling pressure again, heavy pressure."

"You ready to push?"

"Yes!"

"Okay, we go again on three. Dad, grab her leg. One....two....three...puuuusssshh......"

She pushed again, harder this time.

"Okay, dad, Nurse Coleman, pull those legs, we've got the baby's head half way out."

He snapped his fingers to another nurse.

"Take dad's place. I want him to see this."

The male nurse took a hold of Terri's leg and I squeezed her hand before releasing it. I walked around to the end of the bed, where the doctor stood using both fingers and thumbs to stretch Terri's cookie lips wider and wider apart. I stared at the mommy that had brought me so much pleasure, lying there, bloody with a head hanging halfway out. A hairy head at that.

Terri let out a scream and the baby's full head popped out. A face...it had a face, full of blood and slime but still beautiful. The doctor called for a suction bulb and inserted it into the baby's nose and mouth to remove the gunk. Then he said, "Ready mom? Let's get this egg hatched. All right dad, here we go...push mom!"

Terri let out a final scream and the rest of the baby came wiggling out. I saw a flash of white, stumbled back and almost hit the floor. Thank God there was another nurse standing behind to catch me. That was some off-the-wall shit.

"It's a boy dad," the doctor said as he flipped him, gripped him like a football and slapped him one quick time on his behind. Out came the sweetest cry. He placed him down in the nurse's arms and turned to me with a pair of sterile clamps in hand.

"Care to cut the cord?"

"Uh...yeah."

I stood above the baby, and before I cut his cord from his mother, I took a moment to count ten tiny fingers and ten tiny toes. The doctor instructed me on how to clamp and cut the umbilical cord and then sent me to be with Terri while he finished up.

The nurse cleaned the baby, weighing him in at eight pounds, three ounces. I rubbed a wet towel over Terri's head. She was waiting anxiously to see our baby boy, but she was drifting off to sleep. I could only imagine how exhausting that must have been for her.

"You are so beautiful, you know that?"

"Yeah, right," she said. "I know I look like hell."

"Never that."

She smiled.

"Terri, why did you leave like that and stay away so long? Why didn't you at least call?"

I walked over to the window and waited patiently for a response. I looked back at her only to find her sound asleep. I guess my answers would have to wait. I turned to the nurse taking care of the baby.

She took a piece of paper and held it to the baby's feet, which were covered on the bottom in black ink and placed footprints on the paper. I smiled.

She cleaned him off and brought him to me wrapped in a blanket. He was almost white in color. Curly black hair with skin so wrinkled yet so soft. He must have been quite hungry from his journey into the world because he had his entire fist in his mouth. The nurse came to me with a bottle of milk and handed it to me.

"You want me to feed him," I asked.

"It's important in the bonding process. Here, sit down in the rocking chair and I'll hand him to you."

She propped him in my arms.

"Don't be afraid."

He was so small, I thought he was going to slip out but he just snuggled there, like he already knew who I was. I gently kissed his forehead and the elderly nurse assisted me in feeding and burping him. Both he and Terri were fast asleep.

I laid him in the baby bed beside Terri and although I knew I needed to get back to Alicia, I couldn't bring myself to leave. I just stood there, watching him sleep.

"I've waited a long time to see you lil man. At first, I was scared but then the thought of a little me excited me. Then yo' moms took off and I was afraid I would never see you. Funny how life does that, huh? Afraid for you to come, afraid for you not too. Now, here you are. I want you to know that no matter what anybody says, you were created in love."

I looked to Terri.

"And despite all, I do love your mother very much and I love you too."

I picked up his hand with my index finger and he wrapped all of his around mine in return. I almost cried and I held the biggest smile.

"I promise you son...son...I'll never leave you or your momma again. I'm here to stay and hopefully you two are too. I wonder what she's gonna name you?"

"Why don't you do the honors," Terri said.

"Hey, you, I thought you were sleep."

"I haven't seen our son yet. Can you please hand him to me?"

"Sure."

I slowly picked up the baby and handed him to his mother. She immediately began to cry.

"He's so beautiful."

She kissed him; I stood there and watched them.

"Terri, I know we need to talk but..."

109

"Its fine Arman', we can talk tomorrow. Go handle your affairs, we'll be here...I promise."

Terri smiled and I kissed her on the forehead. I leaned over and placed a tender kiss atop my son's forehead also. "I'll be back in the morning. I'll call you as soon as I can. I..."

She looked at me and the tears fell.

"Go," she said.

I walked outside the room and stood there along side the wall. Softly, I could hear her talking to our son. "There goes the only man I've ever loved. I promise you both that I'll be the best mother I can be. I love you little one...and your daddy too. I'm so glad he was here to share this with me and see you come into the world. I wonder if he'll allow me to name you after him."

As I stood there, the tears began to well up in my eyes. There they were...the two people who had stolen eighty percent of my thoughts for the past several months, sitting there...a family incomplete. A body without the head. I couldn't turn my back on them, not now. They needed me too much. More so, I needed them.

I finally tore myself away from the door and headed for my car. I was suppose to call Cory so he could bring the family up to the hospital but that just wasn't the best course of action to me.

I hit the highway and called Alicia's house. Cory answered the phone.

"Yeah, whaddup?"

"Whaddup, man, it's me."

"Nigga, where the hell you been? Momma J is over here ready to buss a cap in yo' ass," he laughed. "And I don't even wanna begin to talk about Punkin and they peoples. Pooh 'nem all here, ready to roast that ass."

"Very muthafuckin' funny, nigga. I just saw a miracle happen playa. I saw my son come into the world. I held him, I fed him, and I even cut the cord from Terri to him. It was amazin'. He's healthy and so handsome, just like his daddy."

"Yeah, well, congrats nigga. You might just be headed back to that hospital stretched out yo' damn self," he said laughing.

"Look, man, just tell everybody I'll be there in ten."
"Cool."

Allysha Hamber

CHAPTER 17

As I rode along, the Alpine pumped out Regina Bell. "...I would teach you all the things I've never learned. Yes I would, if I could..." Protection, encouragement, wisdom and the knowledge of life. Everything I wanted to give my new son, just as my mother gave me.

As I pulled into the driveway, I noticed moms sitting out on the porch. She was obviously waiting for me. As I approached her, I could see the worry in her eyes.

"Sit here, son, beside me," she said as she patted the top step beside her.

"You know, Manni', I've prided myself in rasin' good wholesome kids. You and yo' sista's raised a lil hell every now and then but you were good kids and you's grown into good adults for the most part. You've grown into a fine man, despite ya father not bein' there. We always been close. You never held anythang this impo'tant from me and so I know there's a good reason you chose to keep it to yo'self. I've refrained from jumpin' to conclusions so please, son, tell me what's goin' on round here."

The look in her eyes told me she was very disappointed with me.

"It's like this, momma, me and Terri hooked up one night at the club, when I thought Alicia was interested in Cory and we slept together. We were involved until I found out she was pregnant. I tried to get her to get an abortion. One, cause I wasn't ready for no kids and two I was kickin' it with Alicia."

"Oh, Manni' you didn't..."

"Ma, when I realized our relationship was more than just sex, and that I truly had feelings for her, she was gone. I wanted to be a father to my child but I couldn't find her. I've thought about her all this time and I've wondered where she was and how she and the baby was doing. When I came to the house, I should have told you. I'm sorry, Ma. I told Alicia about her to an extent. I told her it was just a one night stand, but Ma, it was much more than that."

She raised my chin and looked me in the eyes. She always said you could see a person's soul through their eyes. "You love her, don't you, son?"

"At first, I didn't know. I mean, I kept saying to myself how can I love her and Alicia. I..."

"Manni', it's time for' one of life's little funny lessons. Baby, love is a feeling that can be shared with so many different people in so many different ways. Ya father loved me, he did, he just couldn't settle down. He loved you and the girls; he just didn't know how to show it. You can love 'em both Manni' but you can only be in love with one of 'em or neither of 'em."

Lost, I sat still staring at the ground.

"All I know, Ma, is I don't wanna end up like pops. I'm not turning my back on my son. She can't expect me too. I saw him come into this world, Ma. I saw him take his first breath of life. He's so tiny, so soft and so beautiful."

I got quiet. My mind drifted back to the hospital. "How much does he weigh, son?"

"Eight pound, three ounces."

"Tiny? Hell, he's a big'en," she said laughing.

"Well, I guess so," she continued. "You weighed eight-one when you's was born."

She smiled. It was so comforting to see that smile.

"A grandson, huh? I'm a grandma. How's the young lady, what's her name again?"

"Terri and she's fine. Ma, you'd love her. They're both resting. I told her I'd be back in the morning. She wants to name him after me."

"That's somethin' you betta decide fo' yo'self. I love you son and I'll stand by you right or wrong. You can't change this situation, but just memba, that chil' is innocent. He didn't ask to come here. He doesn't have a thang to do with this mess so don't you make him suffa fo' it, ya hear?"

"Yes ma'am."

114

"I'm goin' on home now. Pick me up in the mo'ning so I can see this new granchil' of mines."

She hugged me and placed a loving kiss on my cheek.

"Tell Pooh brang her nosy self on out here and let you clean up this mess. One final word son...gowns, cakes, tux's and gifts can all be replaced. The love you feel both for and from yo' child is priceless."

"Thanks, Ma."

I watched her walk to the car. I felt better knowing she understood and blessed my decision. She climbed into the car and blew the horn. Out came Cory and Pooh.

"Bout time you showed up," she snapped.

"Pooh, not now, please let Ma explain it to you."

"Whatever!"

Pooh put her hand up to my face and walked off. Cory yelled, "Aey. I'll call you tomorrow."

He turned to me, slapped five and said, "Whaddup playa? I hope yo' gear is flame resistant cause to' ass is about to go thru the fire!"

"She that pissed huh?"

"To the highest level of pisstivity! So, what you gon do," he asked.

"I don't know man, figure it all out some how. I know I'm not leaving my son. Alicia's gonna have to accept that."

"Drama...you invitin' drama into an already fucked up situation. Playa, send her back to where she came from. Go in there and get yo' wife, nigga. Think about it, Terri shows up to ruin yo' wedding, not to mention we don't even know how she knew you was getting' married in the first place. She probably never left. Game, man, I'm tellin' you, she came back fo' the money."

"I ain't got no damn money," I snapped!

"Man, we on alert to go to war in the Persian Gulf right now. Nigga, if you go over there and die, yo' ass is worth a quarter of a million dollars in life insurance. And if you sign that birth certificate nigga, who becomes the beneficiary? That kid who you don't even know is yours or not. Don't do it, playa. Don't risk what you got fo' no bullshit."

"I don't know, maybe you right, dawg. Let me go holla at Alicia."

I was so fucking confused.

"Say, nigga, be brave. And whatever you do, don't be dumb and ask fo' no pussy. Just do a lot of damn beggin'."

"Aight, playa."

"Peace."

I walked into a house full of cold stares. Punkin, her parents and Alicia were staring at me, better yet; they were all staring through me.

"Nice of you to finally show up," Punkin said.

"Punkin, Mr. and Mrs. Taylor, I really need to talk to Alicia alone. But before I do, I just wanna apologize to you all. Punkin, I know you helped me to get her back and I'm sorry if you feel I let you down. Mr. and Mrs. Taylor, I know you spent a lot of time and money, I…"

"This isn't about the money, young man," Mrs. Taylor began. "It's about our daughter's heart. She believed in you, she trusted you and for what? You pull this on her wedding day?"

"It was my wedding day too and I wanted to marry Alicia just as much as she wanted to marry me. She knows that deep inside." I looked to Alicia who was staring at the floor. "Now, I don't know how much of the situation Alicia explained to you but I didn't expect this. I mean, I haven't heard from Terri in months. I don't know…but what I do know is that I never meant to hurt Alicia. She means the world to me but I can't turn my back on my responsibility. As a man, I can't do that. What kind of man would she be marrying if I did?" I looked to her moms. "Is that the kinda man you'd put your daughter in the hands of."

"It's okay, son," her father said. Thank you God. At least I was getting through to one of them.

"Not one of us in this room is perfect. This here is just a mess you gotta clean up. All I want is for my baby girl to be happy. She's been through enough."

I knew he was referring to her earlier fight with cancer.

"She deserves to be happy," he said.

"I agree with that, sir, and I wanna make her happy. But not at the expense of my son. He can't be ignored. He deserves happiness too."

"Tu-shay, I agree. I'm sure you'll work this out. Come on Ma. Punkin, you're coming with us."

"Philip, I don't think I should go, my baby needs me."

"She ain't no baby, Velma, she can take care of herself. Let them work this out for themselves. Let's go."

After they both exchanged good byes with Alicia, she followed him out of the door. Once the door was closed, the room was quiet and still. Alicia broke the first word through tears.

"A son, huh?"

"Alicia, I know you know this isn't my fault. I can understand everyone else trippin' cause they didn't know what time it is but you knew this would happen one day. Yeah, it could've picked a betta day but I can't change that. I can only deal with it now that it's here. He's my son, Alicia, and I won't allow Terri to leave with him again. Baby, I helped give him life tonight. I know in my heart he's mine."

"Exactly, Arman', he's yours. What place do I have in all this? Where do I fit into this new life of yours?"

"You fit into everything, everywhere because you're apart of me and we're a team. I can't do anything without your support. Alicia please don't make me choose between you and my son. I know you love me too much to make me do that." I moved closer to her.

"What about her Arman'," she asked as she waved her hand in the air.

"What about her?"

"Where does she fit in? I mean, am I gonna go through eighteen years of baby momma drama? You know she will use that baby to get to you. You know she will. She…"

"Hold up Alicia," I said.

117

"Terri ain't like that. She kept tellin' me to go back and be with you. I stayed because I chose to stay and see my shorty arrive in this world, not because she forced me. Terri knows where my heart is and she respects that. She's not tryin' to come between us, baby. I promise you. We've been through this once, Alicia. I can't take being without you again. Look at me."

From the bay window she glanced my way.

"Don't let this tear us apart. It's not the baby's fault. Don't let him miss out being raised with his father in his life because of choices and mistakes his parents made. He's innocent and he deserves the best and it's my responsibility to see to that. I'd really like to do that with you by my side." I extended my hand to her.

Alicia stood there, fresh tears springing forth. She inhaled and let out a deep breath. She walked towards me and I pulled her into my arms. It felt so good to have her there. She squeezed and I squeezed tighter.

"I love you, sweetheart," I said.

"I love you too, Arman'. Don't worry about the wedding, we can do it again another time."

"Yeah? Just promise me that you will still be my wife."

"I promise. So, what's next? We get an attorney, right?"

"Attorney, for what?"

"To get custody of the baby. I mean, we…"

I released her and looked at her like she was crazy.

"What? You want me to take my son away from Terri? What kind of shit is that? There is no way I'm gonna even entertain the thought of removing my son from his mother. She's his lifeline. No, that's not an option. We'll just have to find some other way to work it out, Alicia." I bit my tongue until I calmed down a bit. "But I promise, I will work it out. Just have a little faith in me."

"Okay, so now what?"

"Well, tomorrow morning, I'm headed back out there to see him. Me, mom's and of course I'd like you to come along."

"Naw. You go ahead," she paused. "I'm not ready."

"You sure?"

"Yeah, it's cool. You go on."

"You want me to stay with you tonight?"

She waved me off.

"Naw, I'm gon' turn in. Punkin should be back and Cory said he'd shoot back through so I'll be fine. You just go, get some rest and get ready for tomorrow."

I kissed her goodnight and whispered a heart felt "thank you" in her ear.

Allysha Hamber

CHAPTER 18

The next morning, I drove the one and a half-hour drive to pick up moms. Pooh was sitting at the brown wooden kitchen table. Moms had decorated the kitchen the old fashion way. The huge spoon and fork set mounted on the wall and the pots and pans hanging from hooks all around the kitchen. She had matching apple theme pot-holders and dishtowels thrown about.

Pooh was reading the Sunday paper and she glanced at me with her nose all turned up.

"So pimp daddy, what's up?" she said.

"Hush yo' mouth gal and get out yo' brotha's business," moms shot back.

I put my arms around mom to greet her.

"It's cool, momma, Pooh's just being her evil old self. PMS'in twenty nine outta the thirty one days of the month."

"Well, if you knew when that hoochie was PMS'in, maybe you wouldn't be in this situation."

"First of all, she ain't no hoochie and second..."

"Hush the both of ya," moms snapped.

"I won't have that nonsense this mo'ning. Pooh, you need to be worried 'bout that gal Kevin done knocked up." Pooh's neck snapped as she rose from the table and walked over to the sink. That was the last thing she wanted me to hear.

"Ooohh snap, so that it," I said.

"And you! You need to be worrin' 'bout this mess you's in. Sit down here an' eat so I can go see this granchil' of mines. By the way, how's thangs with Alicia?"

"As good as can be expected, Ma."

"Good...good," she said as she patted my hand. One thing I'd always love about my moms is that even while she was scolding you, she gave you her love and concern as well. Don't get me wrong, you felt the point she was trying to get across but you also felt her warmth.

During breakfast, Pooh hardly said a word to me but once we were finished, she was the first one to grab her purse and head for the door.

"Lets go so I can hurry up and get back," she said.

"Nobody invited you," I spit out.

"I don't care if you invited me or not. I'm going anyway, lil daddy, so lets bounce."

I gritted my teeth and walked out the door. I knew Pooh. She'd go up in the hospital and start all kinds of crap. When her life is jacked up, she wants everybody else's to be jacked up too. Right on cue, she walked into Terri's room once we reached the hospital and prissed over to Terri.

"Hi, I'm Pooh, Arman's sister. I should've met you yesterday. OOPS, no I shouldn't have because you weren't invited to the wedding. Hmm, how exactly did you find out Arman' was getting married anyway?"

Terri jerked her neck back, looked Pooh square in the eyes and said, "Well, not that's it's…."

"Terri, Terri..pay her no mind. Let me introduce you to my mother."

I quickly moved Pooh to the side to let mom's step by the bed. Mom this is Terri and Terri this is my moms, Ms. Jones."

"Please to meet cha, Terri. Everybody calls me Momma J."
Terri smiled.

"Please to meet you too Momma J."

"And who might this be," she asked as she picked up the baby's hand with her finger. I smiled as he gripped her finger the same as he gripped mine's the night before.

"I'm not quite sure what his name is gonna be yet."

"May I hold him," Mom asked. "Of course. Okay lil man, your grandma's here to meet you."

She handed the baby to moms and I squeezed her arm.

"My first gran'son. Oh, he's so han'some."

"Just like his daddy," Terri said, smiling at me.

"Ump, picture that," Pooh snapped!

"Hush, Pooh, an' get on over here and meet yo' nephew."

"No thank you."

"Chanelle Latriece Jones, take yo' head outta yo' behind right this minute and get on over here and see the beautiful gift God gave yo' brotha and this young lady."

Pooh walked over to mom and just stood there. She stared down at the baby and slowly her frown turned into a smile.

"He really does look like you Manni and..." She turned to Terri. "I'm really sorry for what I said Terri. I'm going through my own hang ups right now. And Alicia really loves my brother and I don't wanna see her hurt."

"I know that she loves him. I didn't even know about Alicia until after I found out I was pregnant. I left town because I was hurt but I never stopped thinking about him."

I hung my head down. I couldn't look at Terri at that moment. In a few but powerful words she let me know that I had hurt her very deeply.

"In fact," she continued. "I love him enough to let him be happy with Alicia. I just wanted my son and his dad to have a life together. I wasn't tryin' to ruin Arman's. I only wanted to share this blessing with him."

"And I fo' one am glad you did," moms said. That, I think, gave Terri the reassurance that she did the right thing. "Yeah, me too. Again, I apologize. I exhaled in the wrong direction. You delivered a beautiful baby boy and I welcome both of you to the family."

"Thank you, Pooh, that really does mean a lot to me," Terri said.

"Me too," I said as I kissed her on the cheek. I turned to my mother.

"May I hold my son now?"

She handed the baby to me and instantly, I fell in love all over again. He began to chew on his fist again and I knew what time it was. I handed him back to his mother. I cleared my throat. "Umm, Terri about his name..."

"We'll leave you's two alone to talk," momma said.

"Naw, Ma, it's cool, you can stay."

"We'll be right outside, son. This here's private."

When they walked out, Terri looked at me with sort of saddened eyes.

"Would you like for me to name him something else?"

"No, no. I'd like my first born to be named after me. There's no other way for me to go. It would be my honor."

"Are you sure Alicia won't mind? I don't wanna cause any trouble."

"It's settled. This little guys name is Arman' Letrey Jones Jr.," I said smiling.

"It's settled," she echoed.

I reached down to kiss the baby on the forehead and on the way back up I glanced into Terri's eyes. Without thinking I planted a soft, tender kiss on her lips. It led to another and another. Before I knew it, I had her head pulled back by her hair and our tongues were dancing together in rhythm. I pulled back.

"What was that for," she asked, wiping the corners of her mouth.

"I…I don't know."

I took a deep breath.

"Natural reaction to being that close to you I guess. It's been a long time, Terri and even though I was at the altar just yesterday, I need you to know that I never stopped caring about you. I thought about you so many nights." My tone changed as I thought back to all the worry and all the nights I lay wondering about her safety. "You know you could've sent word to let me know where you were and how you were doing. I was really worried about you."

"So worried you were at the altar yesterday?"

"That's not fair Terri. I mean, you left without at least hearing me out."

"Oh, I heard you out. I heard you loud and clear. You thought that you were in a fucked up situation, right? So I, solved it for you."

She put up her hand. "Look, Arman', the entire time we were together wasn't real to you."

"How you gon' tell me what was real or not to me?"

"Because you had someone else the whole time. I never sweated you, Arman'. I let you have the streets, hit the club and just stop by and kick it with me whenever you had the time. I never asked you for a commitment because I didn't think I had too. I honestly thought I was the only one you were with. I figured, when you got tired of runnin' the streets, we'd take the time needed to get to know each other on a deeper level. But you were spending that time with someone else. I was so hurt, Arman. I know you're committed now and I respect that. But if there's ever a time when you feel you want to be the head of this family…"

She dropped her head.

"You let me know."

I stood there speechless. What could I say? Everything she said was right. I fucked this up, not her. And if anyone was to blame, it was I.

"Why are you still so sweet to me after all I've done to you? No, I didn't try to hurt you, baby, please believe that. That night I first met you at the club, I had only gone there to meet Alicia. But I thought she was hooking up with Cory so I hooked up with you. Later, well the next day after I kicked it with you, I found out that she still wanted to kick it. You never pressured me for a commitment no, but I should've let you know about her."

"Especially the way I like to get down sexually. I liked to do things to you and you keeping me in the dark took away my choice. For me to decide if I wanted to still be with you knowing about her."

"I feel you on that. And I was wrong. When I wanted to talk to you about the baby you were gone. But not a day went by, baby, that I didn't think of you and my shorty. God knows that's the truth. I wanted; no I needed your forgiveness. I've missed you in my life, and now that our son is born, we're definitely gonna be in touch. By the way, where are you stayin'?"

"I was in at Lynne's."

125

"Not anymore. Moms has a four-bedroom house and no one stays with her. Plenty of room for you and the baby."

"Arman', no, I don't wanna intrude on her like that."

"You kiddin', she'd love to have you. She'd never pass up the chance to spoil her first grandchild. She'll probably try to fatten you up too," I laughed.

"What about Alicia?"

I exhaled. "Let me handle that, you just take care of lil man."

Pooh peeked inside the door.

"Manni, Cory and Alicia are here."

We looked at each other. The moment of truth had finally arrived. How would she respond?

"What's up, playa," Cory said as he slapped me on the back. "Yo' moms went to Walmart to hook shorty up with some gifts and thangs. I gave 'em a couple hundred to help out."

"Thanks, man."

He reached out for Terri's hand. "Hey Terri, how you feelin'?"

She took his hand. "I'm all right Cory, how about you?"

"Chillin' like a world class villian. Oh, these are for you."

He sat down the bouquet of roses next to her bed. Terri raised the baby up so Cory could see him. "Damn, playa, you did that! Oh, yeah, he gone be just like his God father, a ladies man."

"Aye, man, I thought Alicia was with you."

"She is, she out in the hallway."

I walked outside the room and Alicia was leaning up against the wall. She looked as if she didn't get a wink of sleep all night. "Hey you," I said kissing her.

"Hey."

"Wanna come inside?"

"I didn't think I wanted to see him but now I think I do."

I smiled. "That means a lot to me."

I grabbed her by the hand and led her inside. I walked her over to the bed.

"Oh," she said as she extended a small gift bag to me.

126

"I brought the baby a present."

She looked down at the floor. She couldn't put her eyes directly on Terri or the baby.

"Arman', aren't you gonna introduce us," Terri asked.

"Yeah sure." I cleared my throat again.

"Terri, this is my future wife Alicia."

That made her head elevate.

"Alicia, this is Terri."

They shook hands.

"Nice to meet you Alicia. About yeste.."

"It's fine," Alicia interrupted. You have a lovely son. What's his name?"

"Well I.."

"Alicia umm..I decided to name the baby after me."

"What?"

She jerked back and looked at me. "Arman', how could you?"

"Alicia," Terri called. "It's not on paper yet. I can name him something else. After my father, maybe."

Alicia wiped her eyes and walked towards me. "No, no. It's fine. If that's what Arman' wants, then that's what it should be."

She turned towards the door. "Cory can you drive me home please." She looked to me. "Please, enjoy the gift."

I looked down at the bag, called after her but she kept going.

"Once again, playa, congrats. Holla at me when you get to the spot. Terr,i take care." Cory followed behind Alicia and once again we were alone.

"I'm sorry, Arman'."

"No apology necessary. I knew she'd trip and she has a right to. But that was a decision I made and she just have to understand that. You did the right thing by coming back Terri and I'm not letting you leave again. I know she's hurt and I know she loves me, but because she loves me, she should try and understand that I'm not walking out on my son."

127

I walked over to Terri and reached for him. She placed him in my arms and he snuggled there. In my mind, I promised myself no one, not even Alicia, would ever come between me and my son.

Terri opened the gift Alicia left behind. It was a silver handled rattle with an engraving that read. "Well wishes Baby Lambert."

She never expected me to give him my last name, but I'm sorry. This shorty was gonna sport my brand name for life. Eventually, she'd understand. Someday, she'd have to...

CHAPTER 19

Over the next few months, things went up and down on a regular basis. Terri and AJ moved in with my moms and she made it her business to spoil them both. I spent as much time as I possibly could with my shorty.

I'd always ask Alicia if she wanted to come along but she always had other things to do. That definitely put a strain on our relationship. Which gave me all the more reason to shower AJ and Terri with all the love I had inside me. In the process, Terri and I became to close; it was as if we'd been friends all our lives. We did all the parental things together. Doctor's appointments, taking pictures and going to parenting classes.

Slowly, Alicia started to bitch about every little thing. Terri calling, me spending too much time with the baby and me spending too much of my pay check on AJ. True, things were getting pretty tight for me but what was I to do? Let my shorty go without? Never that. Terri couldn't work yet, she needed to be home with the baby. I thought about taking a second job but Alicia wouldn't hear of it.

Cory told me to just go ahead and marry Alicia and then my check would increase because she'd become my dependent. Then I'd be eligible for housing on base and only have the cable and phone bill to pay. My Elauntra was paid off so I'd be cool. I'd get at least a two bedroom, washer and dryer included and a big backyard for when AJ gets older. Plus he'd have his own bedroom in case Alicia came around and I could maybe bring him to stay overnight.

I did still want her to be my wife. I just wish things were the same between us and I could still be a full time father to AJ and a full time friend to Terri. I missed Alicia, her companionship, her love and her trust. I didn't want to lose her; I just wished she'd accept my son. I can't front, I understood her hurt, but when she accepted my proposal the first time, she was accepting my past and at least trying to understand, in my eyes, the situation between Terri and me.

Alicia did know Terri was pregnant and we faced the possibility Terri could show up in the future. Still, it was killing her. It had been a couple of months since we'd made love. She'd shown no interest in it and I thought I would be out of place to suggest. But, if I wanted to hold on to her, I'd better do something. Was I ready this time? Was I as certain as the first time? She'd demand most, if not all of my time. I didn't want that to come between the friendship and partnership Terri and I had built.

I needed to discuss my feelings with Terri. I called and asked her to allow mom the watch AJ and get ready so I could take her to lunch. I asked Cory to cover for me at work.

I took her to the Steak House Restaurant on Jefferson Avenue. It was always crowded around lunch time but I didn't mind the wait as long as I was with Terri. I loved to talk to her.

The waiter seated us at a small oak table by the window. If you look out, you could see the Landing at a distance. I briefly thought of Alicia. That helped me stick to why I was there. I stared across the table because Terri looked radiant. Her hair had grown throughout her pregnancy and her figure had thickened. I was in a daze.

"So, what's on your mind, Arman'?"

"First off, thank you," I said as I picked up her hand.

"Thank you? For what?"

"For being a friend to me. You've been there these past months and I appreciate it so much. You're so good with AJ. A natural at being a mother. I love to watch you with him. He deserves the best and he has the best."

Her eyes watered. "Thanks, Arman', but I know you didn't bring me all the way here to tell me that, I know. Something's on your mind. Arman', you know you can talk to me about anything so spit it out."

I swallowed the lump in my throat.

"Well, you know things have been a little hectic for me lately, as far as Alicia and I are concerned. She's been very distant intimately and very vocal about how much money I've been spending. She's also been complaining about how much time I've been spending with the both of you. I mean, she talks to Cory more than she talks to me."

"Kinda like us, huh," she interrupted.

I chuckled. "Yeah, I guess so. But it's different with us; I mean, we share something special Terri. We have a shorty together."

"That's just it, Arman', we, you and me have AJ not you and Alicia. And as a woman who knows what it's like to be in love..uh, I mean who knows you like I do, certainly I can understand how she could feel a little jealous of you spending all this time with us. She's feeling insecure and I can't say I blame her. What you need to do is get her back on the side of the track she needs to be on. Take a break from spending so much time with us. AJ's young but he knows who you are. Not seeing him everyday for a while won't kill him. And maybe you should stop buying him so much stuff. Between you, Momma J, Cory and Pooh, he's got enough gear to last him a lifetime. He doesn't need new clothes every time he leaves the house. He knows nothing about Air Jordan's for you to be spending eighty bucks on a pair of sneaks every two weeks. Actually," she paused.

"I've been thinking about going back AD," she said

"What? For what? What about AJ?"

"What about him, Arman'? Your moms wants to keep him during the day. You know I never go to the field or run this risk of going on alert for war. Besides, I'll be able to get a house and give your momma back hers."

"Naw, I don't like that. I mean, he's too young, he needs you. Is it money? Terri, I'll take care of you I..."

"Arman', you can't take care of us, Alicia and yourself. I want to go back to work. It'll be a rank and pay cut but I know we'll be fine. Go handle your business. I've never been one to stress you and I never will. As long as you don't allow anything to come between us...I mean, uh, you and AJ."

"Neva, you, uh, I mean, my shorty's always gon' have me around. Have I told you lately how beautiful you are, both inside and out? I never would have known you had a baby a few months ago. Your body has recovered well."

"Oh really? Well I'm glad you noticed."

I squeezed her hand. "Always," I replied.

All the passion and desire I had for her came running to the front line. She was sipping on her strawberry milkshake and my mind flashed back to her lips wrapped around my jimmy. Big pretty, soft pink lips. Remembrance of her jaws, her throat muscles and her talent.

"Arman'!" she yelled.

"Yes, baby," I whispered.

"ARMAN'!" she snapped again.

"Yeah, baby," I said more alert this time.

"Where were you just now?"

"Uh…I was thinking about one day being able to take AJ to the park and play ball." I lied.

"I know you can't wait, but you might wanna let him start walking first."

We laughed.

The perky white blonde haired waitress brought our order to the table. My hip stared vibrating. My pager was going off. It was moms. I told Terri, dialed the house in a panick and hoped AJ was okay.

"What's wrong, Ma? Is AJ okay?"

"Sleepin' soundly child. It's Willie."

Willie Lee Jones, also known as my run away dad.

"What about him?"

"He's in the hospital. They say he on his death bed. Apparently, he wants to see you kids. Pooh's headed up there already. You get on up there too. I'm behind ya'll as soon as Addie Mae get here to watch the baby. Take Terri with you."

"What I gotta go for? I don't wanna hear nothin' he gotta say."

"Arman' Letrey Jones, you get off this phone and hot tail yo' ass up to the hospital befo' it's too late to see yo' daddy. Now he's made mistakes but so have you. Oh, I fo'got you so perfect that you can look down on someone else?"

I was quiet.

"I didn't think so. Now get on up there and you better be there when I get there!"

Click. She hung up on me.

I sat back down at the table gritting my teeth.

"What's wrong?"

"My so called daddy is croakin' and now he wanna make amends. Fo' what, I don't know. I gots no love fo' his ass. He left me when was way younger than AJ and we ain't heard from his ass since. What could he possibly have to say to me?"

"He's sorry. I mean, maybe he wants to just make things right before it's too late."

"It's already too late," I said.

"It's never too late, Arman'."

Terri smiled at me.

"Look at us. I mean, our situation. When I left, I wanted so many times to come back and talk it out with you. It's a good thing I came because look at all we share now."

I sighed.

"Go see him. At least hear what he has to say."

"On one condition, if you come with me."

She smiled again.

"Let's go."

I called Cory and told him.

"You playin' right? Just like black folks, wait 'til they half dead to fix shit and handle business. How he gon' procrastinate 'til he got four seconds for his heart to stop beating?"

"I don't know, man, moms is making a nigga go up there so, I'll get at you later…"

"You want me to bring Alicia up later?" he asked.

"If she wants to come. I left her a message on her machine but I'm taking Terri with me."

133

"You really got a death wish huh, nigga?"
"Peace, nigga."
"Peace."

CHAPTER 20

The hospital was the same one Terri delivered the baby in a few months back. The receptionist at the front door directed me to the intensive care unit on the fifth floor. Pooh was sitting at the end of the grey corridor, waiting for me.

"Hey guys."

We all exchanged hugs.

"How you holdin' up?" Terri asked her as she kissed her on the cheek.

"I'm fine."

"Why you sitting out here," I asked her.

"I don't know what to say to him or what to expect. I didn't want to go in alone. Ma said she would send you so I waited."

"Well, I don't know what to say either but I'm here so lets get it over with."

Terri sat down.

"I'll wait out here for you guys. This is family business."

"Okay, but I won't be long."

The room was filled with machines, tons of lights flashing, codes ringing and equipment everywhere. He was up and talking to the nurse. Complaining about a pain in his back. I stared at him. There he was, about one hundred twenty pounds and shrunk down to around five foot four. He looked like a skeleton with a thin layer of skin on top. His body was so frail. His head bald and his fading mustache was salt and peppered. He looked nothing like his pictures Big Momma use to show me.

When he noticed we were there, he quickly excused the nurse.

"Hello Willie, I'm LaNelle. You remember me? Pooh is what everybody calls me."

He cleared his throat, reached up for her hand and said, "Course I memba you youngin'. I gave you that name. You use to walk around just shittin' all over the place when you was little, so I called you Pooh. Where's Rhonda and Tonya?"

"Tonya's in Cali with her husband and Rhonda's overseas in the Navy. I'm sure mom will let them know. She's on her way too. Until then uh....here's Arman'." He pointed to me.

"Naw, no way, that ain't my son. My boy ain't that tall and han'some."

"How would you know? You ain't seen me since I was born, memba? You walked out on us. What the hell you want anyway? Cause you sick you think we suppose to come runnin' and pouring out forgiveness? Well sorry but I'm fresh out."

He took a drink of water. It looked like it pained him to swallow.

"I know you gon' let a dyin' man see his kids befo' he meets his maker and have to explain why he walked out on 'em twenty four years ago."

"You mind tellin' us before you tell your maker?"

"Manni'!"

It was moms.

"You put yo'self back in yo' place right now young man. I know I didn't raise you with a disrespectful mouth like that."

I chuckled. "You sure didn't ma."

"No matter what he done, he still yo' daddy."

"Not accordin' to him when I was born," I huffed.

"Hush yo' mouth boy, can't you see the man' ailin'?"

Willie held his hand up in the air.

"That's okay Zell, he has a right to be pissed off. Let him blow off his steam."

My mom pushed past Pooh to give him a hug.

"How you feelin', Willie? They say your playin' days done caught up with cha and left you with a bad case of cancer."

"Yeah, it's tryin' to slow me down, but you know me.."

I tuned them out. Didn't wanna hear nothing he had to say. I stepped in the hall to make sure Terri was okay. She was asleep in the chair. I took off my jacket and laid it over her. I kissed her on her forehead. Then I took a deep breath and headed back inside.

When I entered, Willie asked to speak to me alone. Before I could answer, moms and Pooh darted out the door.

"Come on over here and sit down son."

"Arman'," I said flatly.

"What?"

"My name is Arman', not son."

He popped up his hands.

"Well 'cuse me Mista Arman'. Get on ova here, sit down and listen to dis' ol' fool while you still got a chance."

He sighed as I took the seat beside his hospital bed.

"First of all, let me apologize for, walkin' out on the family all those years ago. I left you to be the man of the house. I was young and scared."

"That's no excuse."

"Can I finish?"

I waved my hand.

"Anywayz, I had plans on goin' to California makin' it big playin' tha guitar in a band and comin' back to get ya'll but it didn't work out."

"A band? I never knew you played no guitar. And Ma said you left cause you thought I wasn't yours."

"Oh, that was just some bullshit excuse I gave her cause I couldn't tell her I was really leavin' to pursue a pipe dream. I started playin' at local clubs and with it came the drinkin', smokin' and druggin' more than I already was. I never left Texas, couldn't afford to. Been right here all these years. Seen you mo' than you think I have."

I looked at him confused.

"Seen me? How? Where? "

He laughed. "Short stop, little league baseball for the Tigers. Runnin' back numba thirty two fo' tha Tigers. Three touchdowns homecomin' game in ninety. Runna up fo' homecoming king same year. Sixteenth rankin' U.S. Army graduate from boot camp. I've kept up wit' cha and even though I wasn't there where you could see me, I was there. I'm sorry to tell you afta' all these years, I'ma failure, but I'm proud of you and yo' sista's. Ya'll became good kids, no thanks to me. Well, I guess that's not true. I mean, you used yo' hate fo' me as fuel to keep pushin' ahead and that's cool. Just be carefa' with hate son cause if you leave it inside fo' so long, it will consume you."

"I don't get it, if you were there, why didn't you want me to know? All those years you waste, you cheated us all."

My eyes watered and I was ready to leave. As I rose up, he held his hand out and motioned for me to sit.

"I was a failure at what I sat out to do, son, and I didn't feel I deserved to be a part of ya'll lives. But I sure did keep up with cha. To sickly to make the weddin', though. Shame too, hear I missed a doozy. Gal's poppin' out youngin's and thangs. Yo' momma told me the story, the whole story. So you'd caught 'tween two gals and a hard place, huh?"

I leaned back in the chair and exhaled a deep breath.

"Not really. I mean, Terri and I share AJ. Alicia and I share an engagement. I mean, I love'em both in different ways and for different reasons. Terri's like my best friend but I have an a very strong sexual attraction to her."

He laughed.

"Plus we now share a stronger bond because of AJ, which in turn is leading to more problems with Alicia. She's my world and she doesn't even realize it. I'd give anything to make her happy except I don't know what that is anymore. I was just talkin' to Terri about cuttin' down some of the time I spend with AJ. I…"

"Now hold on, son…Arman', you take it from dis old man, you don't let nothin', I mean nothin' stop you from bein' there with yo' son. You hear? Don't let life, wife or anything else side track you from bein' there for those birthdays and little league games. There isn't a day that goes by I don't regret leavin' ya'll. But my pride wouldn't let me come back."

He stared off at the naked beige wall.

"A lump of pride is like an asshole, son. Everybody's got one. And pride, like constipation keeps a lot of shit inside you and you find yo'self spittin' out shit every time you open yo' mouth. Then everybody's runnin' from round you cause of the smell you leave behind. If this here young lady loves you, she'll accept the mistakes you've made and help you raise yo' son in any way she can. If it's her you really wanna be with then you needs to control yo' hormone's round this other young lady and keep it all about the baby. Ain't nothin' wrong with bein' friends, in fact, I encourage it. Just know yo' boundries. Pussy is every great man's downfall, son, don't let it be yours. Life is a game of chess and chances. Know that you the king, they's the queens and everyone else is the pawns. Neva take chances yo' dick can't cover. It's yo' world but the Man upstairs is only allowing you to rule fo' a spell so do yo' thang and make the right choices. You's the big six domino, son. When and how you's played, always determine the outcome of the game. It all revolves round you. Unda'stand?"

"Yeah, I do." I smiled and reached for his hand. "Thanks," I told him.

The tension was gone. I leaned back again and before I could speak, he was fast asleep. The medicine had him out cold. There he was, the man that I loved to hate. All these years, so vulnerable and needy.

I'd forgiven him, just like that. I decided to spend his final days getting to know him and introducing him to his grandson.

As I sat there staring at him, I could hear my moms in the distance. Gals, get a hold of yo'selves and calm down. You's in a hospital fo' Christ sakes. Folks is sick up in here.

"What's she doing here? I mean damn, is she part of the family? Everytime I turn around, she's there," Alicia said.

"She's the mother of my granchil' so yeah, she's part of the family. But that don't take nothin' away from you chil'. You's gotta be an adult about this situation."

"I've been grown about it," Alicia snapped. "I accepted the fact they have AJ but I'm far from stupid, there's something else going on here."

As I walked out the room, they both looked at me. "What's goin' on out here," I asked.

"You tell me," Alicia snapped again. "Why did you bring her here?"

139

"When momma called me, she was with me at lunch."

I instantly regretted that one.

"Lunch, huh? What's lunch gotta do with AJ?"

Alicia walked over to Terri.

"I know you were just using that baby of yours to get Arman'. If you meant that much to him, don't you think he would've stayed around for more than just a one night stand?"

Terri looked to me and I watched as her eyes reflected the hurt that statement had just caused her.

"How low of a woman are you?" Alicia continued.

"A…Alicia, you're wrong about this. We were just…."

"You're the bottom of the barrel. Any woman that uses her baby to get a man is trifflin', skanchy…"

"Trifflin'? Skanchy?"

Terri stepped back and put her hand on her hip.

"You really wanna know how trifflin I can be? I have taken entirely too much of your bullshit. Remember who had him first, no matter who has him now. By the way, are you bi-sexual?"

Alicia's face turned red and flushed.

"Excuse me?"

"You know, like to screw women? I just wondered cause every time you kissed Arman', you were tasting me…"

"Daammnn," Cory screamed. "That had to hurt!"

POW!! It happened so fast, no one had time to react. Alicia had slapped Terri with an open hand. Terri retaliated and slapped Alicia back. It stung her pretty bad cause she stumbled backwards. Terri was a lot stronger physically, but when Alicia regrouped, she came at Terri like a linebacker from Penn State. She rushed Terri so hard; she knocked them both into the wall. It was hair pulling, wild swinging and loud cursing.

"Damn, nigga, this is straight up cat fight, equipped with acrylic paws," Cory teased.

"Manni', boy do somethin'! Ya'll stop this mess! Oh Lawd Jesus, I'm a have a heart attack," Mom yelled.

I ran over and tried to get in the middle of them. Cory grabbed Terri and I grabbed Alicia.

"Stop it! Calm down! What the hell is wrong with you? Fightin' all up in here like some thug! My daddy is dyin' in the other room and ya'll clownin' over stupid petty shit!"

I grabbed Alicia tighter and she squirmed to get loose. "Alicia! Stop! What's with you?"

She looked up at me, tears running down her face.

"You tell me, Arman', mista one night stand. Are you still sleeping with her? Is that why you haven't touched me in almost two months? You tell me what's going on!"

"Is that what you flippin' fo? I can't believe you would think that, after all we've gone through?'

"Why not?"

She yanked away. "You're always with her and you're doing lunch dates and..."

"Our lunch date...our meeting was, for me to tell Terri that I won't be coming around as much because I know how much it bothers you."

Alicia looked over to Terri, rage still in her eyes. Mom and Pooh was talking to Terri, trying to calm her down. She was so upset. I'd straightened things out with her later. Right now I had to get Alicia under control.

"And," I raised her face. "To tell her I was getting married." Her eyes lit up. "Next week if you're available."

Finally, a beautiful smile came across her face. I hadn't seen that smile in what seemed like ages.

"Really....married?"

"Um-hum," I answered. "What do you say, you available? You still wanna do this?"

"You bet yo' ass I'm available."

We kissed each other in desperation. Trying to hold on to something, I wasn't sure what, but something.

"Let me talk to Terri?"

She shook her head. When I turned around, Terri was gone.

"Ma, where's Terri?"

"She took a cab to get AJ."

"And go where?"

"I don't know son, she didn't say."

I looked at Alicia. "You mind?" I asked.

"Naw," Alicia said.

"We can celebrate later, just you and me," I told her.

"I'd like that."

I kissed her goodbye. As I got to the elevator, the sirens went off in Willie's room. Nurses, doctor's and a slew of people ran inside. Alicia, Ma Cory and Pooh stood at the door, peeping inside.

I rushed past them and tried to get to Willie. A nurse stopped me.

"You'll have to wait outside sir."

I wouldn't move and eventually she got the hint and went on about her duties.

"Hit him with 200 watts," the doctor said as they tried to jump-start his heart with electricity.

"300."

No luck.

"Stand back...start CPR."

It seemed like hours I stood there but in reality, his life slipped away in a matter of minutes.

"Failed resuscitation...time of death, six p.m."

He walked by me and put his hand on me shoulder.

"Sorry, son."

Soon...my dad was gone again. I felt cheated again but I also felt grateful that I got to resolve things with him. Thankful that I got a chance to talk to him. I walked over to the bed.

His eyes were wide open as if he was looking up, amazed at heaven. I held his hand and closed his eyelids.

"Maybe you can't hear me physically but spiritually you can. I forgive you and, I'm sorry, for being so hard on you." I paused to collect myself after hearing the screams from the hallway.

"I can't believe all these years, you watched me grow into a man. I promise, Willie, uh, dad, I'm gonna break this cycle of abandonment that has plagued our last two generations. I'm gonna go get my son and work this all out."

I bent forward and softly placed a kiss on his forehead. I covered his face with his sheet.

"Bye dad, rest in peace."

I walked out and hugged my moms.

"You okay?"

"I'll be fine, son. Willie's gone on to a better place."

I hugged Pooh and gave her a kiss. I turn to Alicia.

"I gotta go get Terri, before she takes off again."

"I'll stay with the family, dawg, go...," Cory said.

I jumped in the car and headed for moms house. How could I let all this blow up the way it did? I had to a grip. I had to make peace some how and make this work between the three of us. As I sped down the highway, the sound's of "When a Woman's Fed Up" in my ear caused me to reflect the words of my father in my mind.

"You's the big six domino son...it all revolves around you."

I had allowed her to get hurt again and the first thing she does at the slightest pinch of pain, is run. I sped up and once I turned the corner, my stomach sank.

I rushed into the house and called her name. I got no answer. I went into the bedroom noticing most of her and AJ's things were missing. I walked over to his crib, reached down and picked up the rattle he'd played with so many times while he rested in my arms. I sat down on the bed.

On the dresser was an envelope addressed to me and as I began to read, the tears fell.

Arman',

You're right, we can't do this. It's not good for either of us. I apologize for the way I acted. It's just her words stung like poison. Maybe, she's right, maybe I was hoping AJ would bring us back together. I knew, from the first moment I saw in that church, that I was still in love with you. But, it's clear that I don't belong here. I've intruded in your life long enough. One night stand, huh? Ouch!

Anyway, when I get where I'm going, I'll let you know. Until then, take care. Please, apologize and thank Momma J and Pooh for me. Don't worry about us, and I hope Willie is okay.

Love,

Terri.

P.S. Congratulations

She was gone again. This time, with my shorty. She promised she wouldn't do this again….Damn.

CHAPTER 21

"...but when you love someone, you just don't treat them bad..."

Donnel Jones took me home that night. I tossed, and I turned. I even made love to Alicia, trying to cover up the hurt I felt. I was sick about AJ, my dad and Terri. Too much to take in one day. Terri was more than just my baby's mother. She had become one of my closet friends next to Cory. Where the hell are you?

I asked Cory to help me find her after Willie's funeral.

"Man, I miss her. I miss my shorty."

"What I don't understand is, why she gotta keep takin' off. Ain't nobody Matlock around this mothafucka. I ain't finna go off investigatin' shit! Burnin' up leave days, missin' pussy to chase her ass all over the damn globe."

"Dawg, just help me man, please."

Cory sighed. He could see the hurt in my eyes.

"You got it, playa. Where do we start?"

For weeks, we checked everywhere I could come up with. She hadn't been in touch with AJ's doctor and she hadn't left a forwarding address anywhere. If she was still in Texas, she was underground. I had given up after about two months. I had to go on with my life.

One day, I'd make sure my son understood that I didn't walk out on him; he was taken from me without a trace. Deep in my heart, I knew eventually she'd come back with my son. Meanwhile I had a marriage to arrange. Alicia deserved that at least. She had truly been patient while I ran amuck trying to find Terri.

We had simply decided to go down to City Hall this time. Cory was my best man. Punkin, her maid-of-honor. Mom and Pooh were our witnesses.

That morning, It was packed and the wait gave me time to think. It had been almost three months since Terri left. She promised she'd get in touch with me. AJ was now eight months old. He was crawling, sitting up and even possibly trying to stand by now. I was missing all that. Why does she always have to run? The anger I felt inside pushed me closer to the altar.

"Mr. and Mrs. Jones," the female clerk called. Alicia's face lit up as Cory slapped me on the back.

"Man, are you sure you wanna do this?"

"Yeah, man, what's wrong? You ain't lookin' right."

"I just, I…"

"What, man?" I asked Cory.

"It's nothin'. I'm just getting' prepared fo' any more broads poppin' up with babies and shit."

"Man, come on," I said.

I was halfway there mentally, knowing deep down I was doing the right thing but struggling to come to grips with losing Terri at the same time.

"I do."

The exchanges came and went suddenly. I had to decide to let the past go and as I placed the ring on Alicia's finger, I vowed to do just that. She seemed so happy and I owed it to her to see that she stayed that way.

We'd rented a room at the same hotel I'd taken her to the night we'd gotten engaged. She'd been feeling a little ill since dinner. I told her to lie down on my lap.

As I stared down at her, I whispered softly, "I love you. I love you and I'm sorry for all the things I've put you through. You've been there through thick and thin and I don't know what I'd do without you."

She rose up to me.

"You're so special," I continued.

"And I promise you won't regret not one day being my wife."

I kissed her and that old magic was there.

"Wait, I've got something for you," I said.

Alicia's face beamed.

"What? What is it?"

146

"Okay, okay calm down. Close your eyes."

She closed her eyes and I produced a long velvet box.

"Okay, you can open 'em."

She grabbed the box and opened it.

"Uhhh….," she gasped. "Arman' it's beautiful, ohhh…thank you."

It was a diamond necklace with a heart at the center. Took all my income tax to buy.

"I chose it because I always want you to have my heart."

"Oh, baby."

I wiped her tears and kissed each cheek, before entering her salty mouth. It was warm inside. A feeling I was all too happy to feel. She pulled back.

"I have something for you too."

"You didn't have too."

"No, fair is fair," she said as she straddled my lap, facing me. Alicia took my hands and put them on top of her stomach. "Feel anything?" she asked.

I was confused.

"No? Well, according to the doctor, you should in a few more weeks."

"You mean…"

"Yes, I mean…I'm pregnant."

"Oh, my God! Are you serious?"

"Yes, baby, I'm serious."

I picked her up and swung her around. I'd missed Terri's pregnancy, I wouldn't miss this one. I laid Alicia down on the bed and fluffed the pillows behind her head. Since she'd told me, I could actually see the small bulge in her stomach. That would explain why she'd been getting sick lately. She lay there, naked and with child, my child.

I rubbed her feet then moved up to her calves. Her body was so soft. I caressed her thighs as I placed gentle kisses on her legs. I crawled between them and stopped at her belly.

"Hey little one, it's daddy."

She began to stroke my head.

147

"I can't wait to see you, to hold you and to love you. I'll always be there for you, you can count on that."

I placed a kiss on her stomach.

"Now, if you'll excuse me, I'm gonna make love to your mother."

I continued my journey up her body to her breast. Reflecting on the hurt she'd suffered because of the cancer. "Are you sure your health can handle a pregnancy?"

"The doctor's are gonna keep close eyes on me."

"But…"

"Shh," she said placing her finger to my mouth. "Don't talk…just make love to me."

I went back to her breast. Nibbling gently as I circled around the nipples with my tongue. I went down to her navel in a swirling motion. Ummm, I wondered what pregnant mommy tasted like. I spreaded her lips to expose her clit. It was sitting out, waiting to be touched. I didn't feel like toying with it, it had been too long. I dove right in with anticipation of the moans and the movements from her body in heat. I clinched her clit with my teeth and placed my lips to her meat. I sucked in my jaws and as hard as I could, I massaged her mommy with my mouth until she had an orgasm. Her body shook but not hard enough for me. I crawled up between her thighs and pushed inside her. She was soak and wet. Her walls were so warm and wrapped around my jimmy like blanket. "Oh, Arman', it feels so good."

"How good?"

"Too good. Make it feel better."

I stroked harder, and harder. She screamed out, "Yes, daddy, yes…Oh shit, the baby."

I stopped. "What about the baby? Can you have sex like this?"

She gripped my ass tightly.

"Over and over again until the doctor says different. Now, enough talk, make love."

As I stroked, I stroked life back into our love. As her body heated up, it warmed my heart all over again. I was back in love again. My pulse raced, my body felt on fire. I gripped her underneath her pelvis and raised it towards me with each stroke. I exploded. We lay there, breath panting, sweat dripping in each other's arms.

"I love you," she whispered.

"Ditto."

Over the next few months, we visited the doctor regularly. One day, I saw the baby's image on a computer. The doctor placed a gook and a microphone shaped instrument on her stomach. I saw fingers, toes, arms, legs and a head. We decided not to know the sex of the baby. We wanted it to be a surprise.

The digital picture made me think of AJ, the day he was born. I became overwhelmingly sad. I missed him and Terri like crazy. I kept trying to block them out but they were there, engraved in my memory.

The doctor told us our child had an eighty-two percent chance of contracting a blood disease from Alicia. Her chemo and radiation treatments had caused her to develop antibodies to her own red blood cells. This was very dangerous for a newborn baby. When I couldn't be there, I made sure she ate right and kept all her appointments, reluctantly Cory took her. I couldn't understand it though; there was some kind of tension between them. Cory didn't come around as much anymore. If we kicked it, I went over to his spot. Alicia never mentioned anything about it and when I questioned Cory about it, he just said, "I'm worried about you, dawg. How you gon' take care of two kids and a wife? Especially if one's sick all the time? I think ya'll should've thought this thing through, that's all."

"She's fine and so is the baby. And technically, I'm not taking care of AJ because I don't know where he is."

"Awwww......"

"What's wrong, man, you aight," I asked.

He was bent over.

"I been havin' a lil pain in the groin lately, nothin' to sweat over."

"You sure?"

"Yeah, I'm cool."

"Aight, well you know I'm headed off to training for four weeks tryin' to get promoted and shit. I'm a need you to take care of Alicia until you come out there. Make sure she eats right and all that. Can I count on you?"

"No doubt, playa. I got yo' back You know we down…"

"Like fo' flat tizes."

We slapped hands.

"Aight nigga stay up and get yo' nutts checked out."

When we finally headed out to the field, for the first time in a long time, I was okay. Well, sorta…

CHAPTER 22

After I returned home from the field early and surprised Alicia with roses and cider, we where on our way to the shower. When I bumped the bed and woke up Cory, who was asleep in our bed with a fever after he'd had surgery. After I'd explained to him about our misfire and the damage we'd done to the back airport lot, he laughed as he reached over to answer the phone. Cory's face tensed up immediately as he looked from Alicia to me.

"Phone, dawg."

I looked at my watch. Damn dawg, who dat? BC?"

He shook his head and looked off as he mumbled.

"Naw, it's Terri."

I looked to Alicia and then to Cory. I inhaled a deep breath and walked over to the bed and retrieved the phone from Cory.

"What is it?"

"Arman', before you hang up please let me explain."

"Explain what, Terri? How you took off with my son without word or notice of where you was goin'? How you got me sittin' worrin' day in and day out about him. What Terri? What could you possibly want to explain to me?"

"Could we not argue about this over the phone? Could you please come to my house tomorrow and let us talk about this like adults?"

"Oh, so now you wanna be adult about the shit?"

"Arman', please."

I looked to Alicia and sighed.

"What's the address?"

Terri gave me the address and I also took down the number where to reach her.

"I'll be there in the morning."

"Thanks."

"Don't thank me yet, you got a lot of explaining' to do."

I hung up the phone and went over to Alicia.

"Drama, you invitin' drama into an already fucked up situation," Cory said. I pointed to him.

"Stay outta this, man."

I looked at Alicia. "Baby, I gotta do this. I gotta go and handle this. He's my son Alicia and I miss him like crazy. I promised him I'd never leave him and I have to go and re-establish that connection with him."

"I understand, Arman', it's okay, really. You go ahead and I'll be fine. Cory will be here to keep me company."

I kissed her forehead.

"But I still get my shower right?"

"You bet," I said.

CHAPTER 23

The next day, I drove the two and a half hour drive to Plano to see AJ. When I arrived Terri was sitting on the front porch with her hair pulled back into a ponytail, looking fine. She was dressed in a blue jean bib short set. She was almost fine enough to make me forget I was pissed off in the first place.

She had a two-story brick home with a huge play yard on the side full of things for AJ. Her garden was full of flowers and roses. When she saw me approaching she began to smile.

"Come on inside."

"Where's AJ?"

"He's at the sitter's, come."

She stood to enter the house.

"Naw, that's okay. I thought...."

"He'll be here in a minute, Arman', come on inside and let's talk."

I followed her inside.

"This is nice. Tight, I like this," I said staring at the crème colored leather living room set with the matching dining room set as well. Beautiful flower arrangements were spread around.

Pictures of AJ lined the walls. My eyes locked on the mantel of the fireplace where a picture of me holding AJ sat in a beautiful silver frame. I walked over, picked it up and traced AJ's face with my finger tips. My anger quickly returned.

"I'm listening."

Terri motioned for me to and come sit beside her with a pat of her hand.

"This is the house I came to the last time I left Fort Hood. My mom owned it and she left it to me when she died last year."

"Sorry to hear that. Willie died the day you left."

"I'm sorry too. Anyway, I left that day because, that day, I saw where your heart really was. You told her I was nothing to you, a one night stand."

"Terri that...."

She held her hand up.

"No, it's alright. It's cool...I understand. My being there was causing too many problems for you. You wanted to marry Alicia and make it work with her and your commitment to us was holding you back."

"How you figure that?"

"Because you had feelings for me and I for you. And as long as I was there, you wouldn't let me go, and I wouldn't have let you go. You know and I know it."

I sighed a heavy sigh. She was right. So maybe this was best, maybe in some twisted way, this gave me the push I needed to do the right thing where Alicia was concerned.

I filled her in on all that had happened since she left. She, in turn filled me in on AJ.

She scooted closer to me, one leg stretched across my lap. "Tell me, Arman'," she whispered. "Have you ever loved someone so much that you'd give your life to see them happy? Even if it's with someone else? To love someone, till it aches down in the very depths of your soul knowing you can't have them? It hurts, Arman'. It hurts like hell. And no matter how much you try to pretend, that you can deal with it, the reality is you can't. I'd watch you with AJ, and each time, I added a little more to my dreams of us being a family one day. That was until you had to leave every night and go home to someone else. I was wrong to stay away so long but I figured that if I stayed away, you'd have the time you needed to save your relationship. I guess it worked out cause look at all that's happened since. It wasn't easy Arman'. As time passed, I watched AJ growing, crawling, feeding himself and every night, I'd put him to bed telling him how much you loved him...." Her voice cracked and her tears fell. "You don't understand how it is..."

She finally broke. Uncontrollably she sobbed as she fell onto my lap. I hugged as tightly as I could and asked her to help me understand. I wanted to be there for Terri as she had been for me so many times.

154

"When I first met you Arman', I fell in love with you. Your walk, the sound of your voice, your eyes, your lips, your entire demeanor...your style. After my marriage, I had such low self esteem, virtually no self worth. I wasn't intellectual or sidity but I was always told I was a master at sex. So I did what I knew best, I seduced you. Then I gave you the space I thought you wanted in your life. But I couldn't even do that right. I led you right in the arms of someone else."

"Terri, you didn't..."

"I was so wrong, Arman'. You wanted intellect and poise."

She rose and looked me in the eyes.

"If I could do it all over again, I'd share with you my love for poetry, for art, for football and tennis. The love I have for nature and my desire to write and sing. If only I'd known."

The tears fell again. I wiped her eyes and I brought her to my chest and stroked her face softly.

"Terri, you never had to pretend with me. You were fine, just being yourself. The night we met, I thought I was just physically attracted to you. You were so beautiful to me. Yes you made love to me like no other woman I've ever been with, but when you left this time, I realized that it was nothing sexual I missed about you. And I'm thankful that we didn't give in to our attraction for each other since the baby's been born because it's allowed me to see that there's so much more between us. I missed the way your hum in the shower, the love you show my moms and my family. I miss watching you bathe AJ and feed him. I missed talking to you and laughing with you. You became one of my best friends. Terri I know there's so much more to you than just sex. You're very intelligent and bright. It takes a special breed of women to date Uncle Sam. You're wonderful baby, both inside and out and I...."

She rushed my mouth and forced her tongue to dance with mine. It was hot and I didn't fight it. I gave in...to all those nights wanting her, missing her, longing for her. All the times I wanted to kiss her gently on the forehead when I swept her hair aside. All those times my heart pumped to love her...I gave in. No thoughts of tomorrow, of tonight even. She had poured her heart and her soul out to me and I received it with joy.

I'd known her love was strong for me but I didn't imagine mine was this strong for her. I wanted her, I needed her, I desired her and I loved her.

She gripped the back of my neck and continued to swallow my mouth. I responded by grabbing her ponytail and releasing the hair from it's clip, letting it fall into my hand. I pulled her head back to expose the neck line I loved so much. I attacked it. Nibbling, munching, sucking and kissing.

"Wait baby, wait," she said pushing her palm into my chest.

"What's wrong," I asked short of breath.

"Nothing's wrong. It's just that I've waited so long for this moment I want everything to be right. Just give a minute."

She looked into my soul, pleading with me to do this her way. Terri had just told me sex was what she felt she was all about. I'd show her differently. She rose up off the couch after I agreed to let her take the lead.

Terri walked into the bedroom and closed the door behind her. Right about then, I would've expected a second thought to creep into my head but none came. The want, the need had been inside me for so long. The need to be with her intimately, it felt both natural and right. The door cracked and she waved for me to come inside.

My heart raced with anticipation as to what awaited me on the other side of the white wooden door. The gateway to paradise. The lights were low, the candles lit on each side of the bed, draped in gold satin sheets.

She led me by the hand to the bed and propped up the pillows before shoving me down. She took the remote to the TV and a smile came to the corners of my mouth. Chris Tucker and Jackie Chan came across the screen. Our first date. She hit the play button on the CD player and out bumped, "If Only for One Night " once again. "....I won't tell a soul, no one has to know. If you want to be totally discrete...."

She returned with strawberries and oil.

"Lets see if we can start all this over," she said letting her gold silk robe fall to the floor. Little did she know that I would be doing all the seducing tonight.

She stood there in a silk gold teddy caressing every curve to her body. My mouth watered. She was stunning. She slid a knee between my legs and leaned into my ear.

"Take it off."

Terri sat down on the bed and watched as I removed my Phem jersey and jeans along with my silk Mickey Mouse black boxers. "Ummmm," she moaned. She reached for my hand and I pulled her up to me.

"Turn around," she instructed.

I spun her around and let my jimmy rest comfortably on her butt cheeks. I released her hair from her neck. I began to place soft kisses on the nape of it.

"You smell beautifully."

I talked to her while searching her body for soft spots to make her tingle.

"Terri, you're the most intriguing creature I know. You're so gorgeous, so funny and so fucking sexy. There's no way anyone with a heart can't see the love you have inside you. Love that's dying to be shared. I've never known anyone with your fire and desire to please. That is until now. Right now that is my desire, to please you in every way. Never second guess your poise, your style or your grace. Your very essence is alluring and your smile alone is worth more than sex could ever be. I've missed you so damn much."

She spun around, face soaked with tears.

"I...," she began.

"Shh, no talking tonight. It's my night tonight. Lay back...."

I laid her down on her stomach.

"...And enjoy."

I took the oil she brought and poured some into my palms. I rubbed my palms together to heat up the oil and began to intensely rub her calves and thighs. They were so soft and tender. She kept her self in good shape.

I applied more oil and moved on to her butt cheeks. For the first time, I noticed the deep groove in her back, it was extremely sexy. I ran my tongue down her back and continued between her butt cheeks. Her body flinched.

As I continued to massage her muscles, I continued to tease her rectum with my tongue. Her body squirmed and her moans gave approval. I brought my hand down and spread her cheeks apart to expose the soft pink opening to the secret garden most men only dared to dazzle inside. I curled my tongue to strengthen it and pushed it inside. Her moans became a scream demanding for more.

The taste of tangy nectarine kept me interested, along with the tightening of her thighs. That meant a climax was near. Not yet. I withdrew my tongue and ran it up her shaking spine.

"What's that all about," she panted.

"Shh. You're talking again. Turn over."

Kevon Edmonds was heating up my mental oven, baking the thoughts of sexing her down with his soultrous voice. "...Every morning you rise and open you eyes, I just wanna be there with you..."

I moved from her stomach to her breasts. So ripe and plump. She could take no more. I twirled my tongue around each nipple before biting them gently. Then I tightly gripped each one, sucking on them with a deadly force. Breast feeding my hunger for her. She jerked, she arched her back and she cried for more. I moved my hand down between her legs. Her juices were flowing like a river. With one strong grip, I pulled on her clit and she screamed.

"Oh, shit that feels good, baby. Do it again, do it so I can let go."

"Naw, baby, that would be to easy. I want it to burst when it finally comes."

I reached over to the table for the strawberries. As I slid between her legs I placed a strawberry inside her mommy and then inside my mouth. Ummm, a flavor even Seagram's' couldn't capture. I did another and shared it with her as we kissed. It turned us on tremendously to share her juices together.

Terri grabbed my arms, trying to pull me to her.

"Please, Arman', make love to me."

I didn't answer. My tongue was playing hockey with her clit. I sucked, I bit and I teased. I entered inside her walls with a mixture of tongue and fingers.

Her hands gripped tighter and I felt her nails dig in. I pulled away, grabbed my jeans and pulled the belt from inside them. I tightened the belt enough to where she couldn't get loose. It was kinky, it was exciting and it was also so she couldn't scratch up my back and leave evidence.

I spread her legs apart and guided them up to her stomach and onto my shoulders. With the tip of my jimmy, I massaged her clit and her lips. Her moans were uncontrollable. I put the head inside only to take it out. Again I entered and exited. It was like a sauna so hot and steamy. With a curved stroke, I plunged deep inside as R. Kelly's, "Greatest Sex," played on the stereo. "......baby your love stays constantly on my mind, this is the greatest sex I've ever had...."

Each drum beat was met with a down stroke. She screamed like I was killing her, yet she begged me not to stop. She shot one off, then another, and oh yes, another before I finally buried deep inside her, underneath her cervix and filled her with a year's worth of want and need.

I fell down upon her. I was breathing so hard. I untied her and lay beside her. She cried in my arms.

"I love you," I said in her ear. She lifted her head, eyes wide.

"Did you just..."

"Yeah, you heard me. I love you, Terri. Always have and I always will."

The tears fell again. Harder this time. I hugged her tightly.

"By the way, my favorite sport is football too."

We laughed and cuddled so intensely we drifted off to sleep. There was a knock at the door.

"I'll get it, relax."

She left the bedroom and returned a few minutes later with AJ in her arms. He had grown so much since the last time I'd seen him.

"Looks who's here AJ, it's daddy."

My face lit up and I sat up and reached for him. His eyes danced at the sight of me. He remembered me. That warmed my heart and put all my fears to rest. She laid him down in front of me.

"Let's get rid of some of these clothes. You're sweating, baby boy."

He was reaching for me, trying to sit up. She stripped him down to his pamper and let him loose.

"Da...da...da..." Terri smiled.

"What did he say? Did you hear that, Terri?"

She laughed. "I think he wants his da-da."

He crawled up on me as he repeated the syllables.

I swooped him into my arms and my heart melted.

"Hey, lil man. I've missed you so much. You've gotten so big. Momma's taken good care of you."

He rubbed his eyes and kept putting his head against my chest.

"I think he's a little tired," Terri said.

"I've got just the thing for him," I said as I stood with him lying on my chest. I began to slow dance with him to Charlie Wilson's, "Without You."

Terri was in heaven watching us together and so was I. By the end of the song, he was out cold. I took him over to the bed and tried to hand him to Terri but he started to cry. I laid him back upon my chest and lay down beside Terri. She snuggled in one arm and AJ inside the other. She was right, this was heaven and the angels sang us all to sleep.

CHAPTER 24

Maybe it was because she was now carrying my seed that Alicia asked no questions about my visit with Terri that next day, nor any future visits. I went to see them every Saturday morning and returned early Sunday morning.

Terri and I had developed a relationship beyond my wildest expectations, as we watched AJ grow together. For the first time in a very long time I felt happy and I felt complete.

As for Terri and I personally, she never demanded anything, which is why I showered her with my love and attention whenever I was in her presence. Moms and Pooh were more than happy to visit her and the baby with me once a month. They loved her to death and they still gave Alicia the love and respect due to her as my wife.

Never was there a time when another man popped over while I was there. I never arrived and she had company. Our time was our time and it was always uninterrupted.

One evening, we were lying on the couch and my pager went off. It was Cory.

"Whaddup?"

"Pack it up and bring home. Alicia's in labor."

"What? She's barely eight months."

"Yeah, but it's goin' down now, man. She called me and I brought her to the hospital. Bring it on, you ain't got long."

"I'm on my way."

I hung up the phone, told Terri. She virtually pushed me out the door. I kissed both and was on my way.

When I arrived and the L & D ward, Cory was in the delivery room with Alicia. I suited up to join them but I was too late. When I opened the door to the private suite, Cory was wiping his head with a towel. Six to seven people were doing al sorts of things to Alicia. I traced for room for the baby, my baby. They were inserting tubes inside its tiny arms.

"Oh, Arman', baby, I'm so glad you're here."

I rushed to Alicia's side.

"That shit was deep," Cory said as he slapped me on the back"

"I'm here baby, I'm here. What happened?"

"The doctor says the kidney infection I've been battling caused my water to break. She's..."

"She? It's a girl?"

"Yes, sweetie, it's a girl."

I left her conversation hanging and walked over to the table where they were taking footprints from her.

"Dad?"

"Yeah."

I wiped the sweat from my palm and shook his hand.

"We tried to wait on you but this little lady had other plans. She's five pounds, six ounces. She looks healthy but we're concerned about her blood counts. We're gonna need you to go down to the lab on the third floor and give us a few pints."

"No problem, I'm on it right now."

I waked over to Alicia and Cory and told them what the doctor had said to me.

"I'm so sorry, Arman'," Alicia said wiping her tears.

"This isn't your fault, baby; you don't have to apologize for giving me such a beautiful baby girl. Look at me."

I pulled her chin up.

"Everything's gonna be fine. She'll be fine. Daddy's here and once she gets her daddy's blood in her system, she'll be good to go. Okay?"

She looked to Cory then to me.

"Okay."

I kissed her forehead. When I turned to leave, they were placing the baby into a plastic bubble like tank.

"Why is she in there?"

"This here's an incubator. It's made to keep premature babies warm and sterile."

He pointed to this quarter sized hole on it's side.

"This hole is where we'll feed the baby her oxygen. The little band aide on her finger is really a transmitter that will keep us updated on her 02 stats, pulse and respiration. Only the nurses will be allowed to remove her and feed her at this time. She'll spend a few days in the NICU until we can get her transfused and stable."

They wheeled her over to Alicia's bed. Alicia placed her hand to the glass and cried.

"I want to hold my baby."

I grabbed her and nodded for them to take the baby.

"Hey, hey clam down sweetheart. It's okay. Don't worry okay? Matter of fact, don't worry about anything except what you're going to name this little angel."

She calmed down a bit. I pushed her hair from her face.

"C, you stay with her. I gotta go give this blood."

"You got it, playa."

When I returned, Cory was gone and Alicia was asleep. I slowly brushed back her hair and she awakened. "Hey, lovely, I'm back. Where's C?"

"I don't know, he was here. I must've dosed off."

I sat her up on my chest.

"You okay?" I asked her.

"I'm fine. I decided on a name for the baby."

"You did?"

"Um-hum." She answered.

"So, tell me."

"Armani' LaNae Jones."

"Armani'....I love it. I love you too."

We shared a kiss before I excused myself to call and inform Pooh, Terri and Ma of all that had transpired. They all sent their prayers for the baby and Alicia.

When I came back Alicia had fallen to sleep again. I knew she was exhausted so I let her rest. I was a little tired myself. AJ had worn me out earlier and giving all that blood made it worse.

I sat down beside Alicia to catch a nap; I was awakened by the nurse telling me that the doctor wanted to see me in the NICU. I ran down the grey hallway and over to Armani's incubator.

"Is she okay?"

"She's fine Mr. Jones, but we have a problem. We can't transfuse her with your blood."

"Why not? The lab took plenty."

He had a disturbed look on his face. Bad news was on the horizon, I could feel it.

"It's not compatible with the baby's blood. You are a Type B negative and the baby is a Type A negative."

"What the fuck does all that mean?" I yelled.

"They don't match," he said. I stood still in fear. My heart sank and I became enraged.

"So break this shit down for me cause I'm not understandin'! There must be a mistake! Do it again!"

"We did."

He placed a hand on my shoulder.

"In fact, we tested it three times. It doesn't match. I hate to be the one to tell you this soldier, but this baby girl isn't yours. I'm sorry; I didn't want to tell you in front of your wife."

With that, he walked away. I stood there staring down at the tiny baby girl, struggling to survive. The baby girl I could no longer help nor call my own. I opened the door to the incubator and touched her small soft hand. The tears fell. What the fuck is goin' on here? How can you not be mine?

I felt confused, lost, betrayed and in rage. I closed the door and proceeded down the hallway to Alicia's room. I stood outside the door pondering whether to go inside or just walk away. I had to know what the hell was going on. I opened the door, went into the bathroom to wet a towel. I dabbed it across her forehead.

"Hey baby, how's the new daddy?"

Her words stung like a swarm of angry bees. My eyes flinched, my jaws tightened but I had to get a grip. I managed a smile.

"I'm fine. As a matter of fact, I just left that little princess of ours."

"How is she?"

"She's not doing too well."

She sprung up.

"What's the matter? Didn't they transfuse her? I thought she was gonna be alright?" Alicia asked in a panic.

I rose from the bed and walked over to the window. It was bright outside but it was dark in my heart.

"Arman', talk to me," she insisted.

"No," I said softly.

"No what?"

"No, they didn't transfuse her. They couldn't, you see if they had her body would've rejected my blood because our blood types don't match. Why do you suppose that is Alicia?"

She didn't respond. I swirled around.

"Answer me dammitt!!"

She just gazed off into another world. I stormed over to the bed, grabbed her by her shoulders and began to shake her. "Dammitt talk to me! What the hell is goin' on here? Why don't my baby's blood match mine, Alicia? Who damn blood does it match?"

Her tears fell, her words uttered. "It can't be..."

"What can't be?" I asked her.

She looked at me. "It's a mistake."

"It's no fuckin' mistake, Alicia! They did it three damn times! Now, cut the bullshit and tell me whose baby it is!"

She saw the rage in my eyes. My chest was going a mile a minute. She was afraid. She should have been. At that moment, I wanted to hurt her something awful.

"The day of our wedding, when you left me standing there to be with that bitch while she had the baby, I was devastated. I thought it was all over. Even after we had talked it out, I felt we were done. That she'd win in the end because she had your child. After everyone left, I went into the bathroom and got Punkin's sleeping pills from the medicine cabinet. I was confused, I was distraught and I was hurt. So I wanted to end it all. Cory came in and took the pills from me and flushed them down the toilet."

I spun around so fast her body jerked.

"He put them in the toilet, took me in the bedroom and held me as I cried it all out. After that, it happened."

"What happened?" No response. "What happened?"

"We slept together."

Before I knew what had happened, I'd slapped her.

"What?" I snapped as Alicia's hands flew up to guard her face.

She was crying fiercely.

"I hated you for leaving me there! In my mind I was getting back at you. It wouldn't have mattered who it was, I just wanted to hurt you in my mind."

She was sobbing uncontrollably. I backed away, turned and punched the wall. She was right, I had taken her through hell and I didn't have the right to be upset with her. But Cory...down like fo' flat tizes....my ass! My boy since day one. How could he betray me like that? He'd wanted her from the beginning and had taken advantage of her in her most vulnerable moment.

Hold the fuck up, AJ is over a year old now. She's eight months along.

"What the fuck? How many times did you fuck him? How long has this shit been going on under my damn nose Alicia? Talk!"

Through the slob she whispered. "Since that day."

"What?" I had to move away from her cause I was tempted to slap slob from her once again.

"You spent all your time with that tramp and that baby! You never touched me! You never made love to me! You neglected me for them! It wasn't him I wanted, it was you but you weren't available! You were always with them! But when you asked me to marry you I cut if off. He hasn't touched me since."

"Oh, so you fucked him up until the night before we got married?"

"That's not fair."

"Fuck fair Alicia! What's not fair is that there is a little baby girl in there, fighting for her life, that I fell in love with the first moment I saw her and she's not mine!" My temper rose again.

"I can't believe you! He wasn't too much of a dawg ass nigga now was he? By the way, how did he like your deformed ass titty?"

POW! She slapped me. I just exhaled and continued.

"I can't believe I was such a fool. My best friend, my best man and my son's godfather. He was always there to take you to your appointments. More than willing to come by and check on you."

I chuckled.

"No wonder he wanted me to talk you into an abortion."

My blood boiled, my adrenaline raced. I had to find him. I had to kill him.

"I'm outta here!"

"Arman' wait, please!"

I turned back at the door, looked at Alicia and walked out as she screamed behind me.

I got into my car and sped off for his barracks. As I drove, I thought of our lives together. Little league, the football games, high school, our careers and our women. How I had looked up to him my whole life.

I pictured him smiling on our wedding day. The diamond earring he gave me that I was faithfully still wearing. I ripped it out my ear, lowered the window and tossed it.

It meant nothing to me. Every word he'd ever said to me didn't mean shit at the moment. All except these, "Ain't no hoe I can't pull, believe that."

I sped up, hit the corner and there it was. I saw it but I couldn't avoid it....BLAM....it was over....

169

EPILOUGE

In the distance I hear sirens...the lights flashing through the shadows of the leaves on the trees. My vision was blurred. Terri and AJ's face flashed before me. Mom, Baby girl Jones and even Willie. His words ringing in my ear. "You's the big six domino. When you's played and how you's played determines the outcome of the game."

No matter what position of authority you're in, husband, boss, father or preacher, all decisions you make affect other people. Whether good or bad, I chose to date two women at once and ended up with one pregnant. I chose to stop using condoms with Terri. I chose to marry Alicia knowing it wasn't truly what I wanted deep in my heart. I chose....freedom of choice is most always taken for granted. I chose to get into this car full of rage and now those I love most in life will be forced to go on without me. I did exactly what I promised I'd never do....I let someone come between me and my son.

Damn, I can't hear the sirens anymore....it's dark, so dark. I see Willie. Take your hand....should I be afraid? DAMN!

Printed in the United States
45912LVS00008B/151-183